BOUNDLESS

A Historical Novel Based on the Life of

Ann Fielding

Born 1778

Linden Fielding

Narrative Architect Literary House
Email: info@narrativearchitectliteraryhouse.com
Phone: 1-307-271-8373

ISBN: 978-1-964167-38-1 (sc)

CONTENTS

INTRODUCTION

Our ancestors had thoughts, feelings, and ideas that are essential to who they were and what kind of personalities and relationships existed. This book attempts to show a more intimate side of these great people. Ann Fielding was born in 1778 near the town of Oldham located about 5 miles from Manchester, England. It was the beginning of the Industrial Revolution. Spinning thread and weaving the cotton thread into cloth was moving from individual cottages to multi-story mills. The introduction of the steam engine to provide power for the mills greatly increased the demand for coal, which was plentiful in the area. With the power of the steam engine, large machines were invented which radically increased production of cloth. During the 1800's, England, and specifically the Liverpool-Manchester-Oldham corridor of England produced more cotton cloth than anywhere in the world.

Ann and her siblings were orphaned at three years of age when both her father and mother died from separate causes in the same year. Living with an uncle, she was mostly left to raise and teach herself and her younger brother, John. This book tells the story of her determination and struggles to make something of her life. Many of the events are factual and have been documented. The daily life, motivations and conversations are a product of the author.

"Ann" was a common name at the time and in this family. There is another Ann introduced later in the story. If this were pure fiction, no writer would do that to his readers. But, this is also history. The people and names are actual. As a term of respect, the mother will come to be known as "Miss Ann", the girlfriend is "Ann", and the Ann added later will be "Annie".

CHAPTER

1

Ann was late. Late in several ways. The sun had yet to rise above the eastern horizon, but she was already late. She'd been out too late the night before, laughed too much, drank more than she'd promised herself she would enjoying the attention of a coworker from the mill where she had been hired only a few months ago. She woke up this morning nauseated and vomiting. That had been happening a lot lately. She thought it was because of the drinking then realized it didn't seem to matter if she had been drinking or not. Maybe it was something she ate. Maybe she was getting sick. Maybe… it was something else. She worried but had no time to think about it now. Ann, who was barely 18, fixed a small bowl of mush with a little milk. That seemed to calm her stomach for now. She hurried to get dressed and fix a bite of breakfast for her brother, John. While he ate, she fixed a lunch for her and her brother. It was 1796. Ann worked in a nearby mill spinning loose cotton into thread.

In a few minutes, the sun would peek through the three-story brick mill buildings. The new mills built in the town of Oldham, had smokestacks reaching 100 feet or more in the air over the English town, with the number of mills reaching into the hundreds. It seemed a new building was starting every month. This was becoming the epicenter of the world's spinning and weaving industry. Oldham, nearby Manchester and the surrounding towns had all the right ingredients for the budding cotton boom. It was an easy freight haul from the seaport of Liverpool. Bales of cotton arrived from all the major cotton-growing areas of the world including India, Egypt, Africa, and with growing volume, the new country of the United States. Labor was plentiful and millwork, while tedious and dirty, paid well enough to push the standard of living higher. The steady work attracted a steady stream of workers into the area. The work was above ground as opposed to the coal mines. However, the coal mining industry was growing as well since coal was needed to fire the steam engines that were being installed to power the mills. Coal was abundant, nearby and added to the demand for dependable labor. Millwork in this area was divided between the spinning of the cotton fibers into thread, performed mostly by women, and weaving of that thread into cloth, performed mostly by men. Working with the looms with the battering and manhandling of the heavy bolts of cloth was mostly by men, who could withstand the rougher work.

Ann was late fixing breakfast for her brother who worked on a nearby farm. There were just the two of them. They had been completely on their own since shortly after Ann went to work in a cotton mill at age 14. They had been orphans for as long as Ann could remember and had been living with an Uncle, Jim. Ann's father, Tom, had been a miner. He died in a mining accident shortly after John was born when a loaded coal cart jumped the track and crushed him against a wall. The accident left Ann's mother, Betty, with four children to care for: Mary, 11; Susan, 6; Ann 2; and John, who was nearly a year.

Betty went to work in a mill spinning bales of cotton into thread to earn money, leaving Mary to tend and care for the other children through the day. The 12-hour work days, six days a week left little time to care for house and children. Then Ann's mother died of complications from an infection. She had cut her hand badly while peeling potatoes. With four children, no husband, and using her hand in the spinning process, it soon became infected. Betty didn't take sufficient time to care for the injury and the infection became worse, then spread to her lungs. By the time the doctor was called in, it was too late. She grew delirious, her fever increased, and she died. With the death of Betty, the children went to live with Uncle Jim to keep from being sent to an orphanage. With his own children to care for, the extra children were left to raise themselves. They had one bed for the 4 of them to sleep in and barely enough food to keep them growing.

A little over a year later, another uncle, Samuel, agreed to take the two older girls, Mary and Susan, into his home to give needed help for his ailing wife and help with the housework. At least this relieved some of the crowding.

Ann was the only mother John ever knew. Neither of them could remember anything about their parents. What they did know was only what Uncle Jim told them. When Ann was about 12, she and John spent most of their days in the neighborhood, exploring. No one seemed concerned if they were gone most of the day, as long as they made an appearance again before sundown. Uncle Jim had told them about the house they lived in when they were born, which had sat empty since Betty's death. Ann was curious to find it, and over several months asked Uncle

Jim veiled questions hoping to find its whereabouts. She knew it was not far away. But being so young when she left, she had no idea where it was.

"Uncle Jim, was there a river or creek near our old home?" asked Ann one day.

Jim closed his eyes and tipped his head back as if that helped to clean out some dusty corners to help find and retrieve the needed memory. "Yes," he began slowly allowing the image to brighten and come into better focus. "I think it was the Beal River if I remember right. Your Pa and I would head down there on a summer day when we were youngsters and spent the whole day fishing. Then, after a spell, we'd get hungry and build a fire to cook some of the fish we caught. We'd nap for a good share of the afternoon until the sun started getting low before heading home. Oh yeah, you wanted to know if the river was near the house. Not far, about a quarter mile down the road from the house. What was the name of the road? Beal comes to mind. But that was the name of the river. I've got it. It's where Beal River crosses Beal Road. How could I forget that?"

Uncle Jim was revved up now. "When I got married, there were still several of my brothers and sisters at home. So, my new wife and I moved out. But by the time your Pa got married, most of us were gone from the house and our parents were getting in bad health, so he and your Mum stayed there to care for them. Not long after, you kids were born." Uncle Jim got very sullen; he continued, "Then the accident happened that killed your Pa. Your Mum got so worn out trying to keep up with everything, she didn't last long after that." There was a full minute of silence. Jim inconspicuously wiped a tear from his eye and cleared his throat,

"When your Pa and I were teenagers, the river was a magnate. It was our favorite place to take the girls we were palling around with. We use to..."

"That's OK," interrupted Ann, "We don't need to hear about that."

"Oh, yah, I guess you don't," replied Uncle Jim. He immediately halted the conversation, as if he had suddenly remembered who he was speaking to. Ann had accomplished exactly what she wanted. She had extracted some details about where her family home was, and where she and her brother had been born.[1]

CHAPTER

2

Ann was careful to remember the details of where the house was that Uncle Jim had described. Over the following days, Ann and John walked up and down Beal Street. There were several empty houses in the area Uncle Jim had mentioned. After looking them over, they finally picked the one Ann felt was the most likely. They took their time walking around the house several times, peering into the dirty windows.

"Do you think this is the right house?" asked John.

"I can't say for sure," Ann replied, "I was only three the last time I was here. I vaguely remember being scooped up by some man. Several others who were with him grabbed a chair and a mat that I slept on, and we quickly and quietly walked out and shut the door. I remember thinking 'Where's Mamma? We can't leave without Mamma.' As the man closed the front door, a green door, again I thought, 'We're leaving Mamma.' That's it! Let's check the front door."

They rounded the corner of the house and walked onto the porch, there in front of them, dirty and weather checked, was an unmistakably green door. Ann couldn't help but grab John and give him a big hug. They had found their home, or at least it appeared so at this point. With a note of accomplishment in her voice, she said, "Let's see what it looks like on the inside. I wonder if it's locked." It was, but nothing was going to stop them now. They walked around to the back door. Locked again. Then they started walking around the house, checking windows to see if they could get one open. They found one that, with the right size stick, they could pry open enough to jimmy the latch and get it open further. John found a dead bush, broke off several branches of different sizes and took them back to the window. The first branch was small enough to fit but broke as soon as Ann started prying. Using a little bigger stick and jamming it hard into the crack in the window frame, they could pry it open some more. While Ann held pressure on the prying stick, John took a smaller stick, fed it through the space Ann was creating and pried the latch open. The window opened more, but the hinges were rusted and the window bound up. Ann thought it was open just enough to let John scrape through. Ann, being a little older and stronger, lifted John up enough to stick his head through the opening. Now he was stuck there, head and shoulders in the house, but feet outside and off the ground so he couldn't get any footing to push himself inside.

"I'm stuck," he wailed as his legs kicked frantically in the air.

Ann was about to panic when she dropped down on hands and knees and hollered back at him, "Stand on my back. Maybe that'll help you get in." The plan worked. He could push himself far enough through the window, then squirmed the last bit and drop headfirst onto the floor. He lay on the floor dazed and out of breath. "Open the front door," Ann said in a muffled holler, not wanting to attract attention from anyone who may be passing.

As John walked to the front door, the stale, musty air, mixed with the stench of decomposing dead mice caused him to hold his breath as he fussed with the lock on the door. Finally getting the door open, he stumbled out, inhaling big gulps of fresh air.

"It doesn't smell too good in there," he said. They decided to leave the door open and sit on the front step for a few minutes to let the place air out. "Now what?" he finally said, looking over at Ann, who was looking quite pleased with their accomplishment.

"Let's give it a few minutes, and then let's see what we can find," she replied. It didn't take long for curiosity to move them inside. "Let's open the back door too so maybe we can get a breeze through here."

The house had only two rooms downstairs, a kitchen and what appeared to have been a bedroom. A table and stool were the only items in the kitchen, and what Ann guessed was a stove. Ann had never seen one quite like it before, but a connection to a chimney confirmed it was a stove. It was a simple square box with a flat top and a pipe to the chimney out the back. John opened the door in front and found it half full of clinkers and charcoal. The flat top could heat up a pan or kettle.

"If we were the last ones to live here, maybe we can find something that will confirm this is the right place," Ann said as they continued to poke into corners.

But there wasn't much of anything but dust and mouse droppings. Ann focused on the table. It had the usual scrapes and scratches that came from using it for everything from de-feathering and cleaning a chicken to having Sunday dinner on it.

"I know a few letters, is that an F scratched on the leg of the table?" questioned Ann.

Neither Ann or John could read or write. Due to the natural curiosity of a child, Ann had picked up the shape of a few letters, especially A and F, her initials. She noticed the F in the table leg.

"John, our last name is Fielding. That starts with an F. Maybe it was someone in our family that put it there." Now they were both looking intensely at a few letters scratched on the table leg.

Ann continued, "What is that bumpy letter just before it. I don't know that one. Look at it closely, remember it, and we'll ask Uncle Jim if he knows what it is." Then Ann remembered Uncle Jim didn't know they had been looking for the house. She added, "Let me ask him about it. Don't you say anything. I need to ask in such a way he doesn't get suspicious of where we've been."

They wandered into the bedroom. The only piece of furniture was a sleeping mat big enough for two people.

"I'll bet this was Mum and Pa's bedroom. Think about that a minute, two people, our parents, which neither of us ever knew, probably slept on that mat. Mum probably got sick and died in this room." Without realizing it, Ann had stumbled onto a detail that was scary and at the same time, made them feel very somber but respectful of the history of where they stood.

"Do we have older brothers or sisters?" John asked, breaking the silence that had settled into the room. "I remember a couple of years ago, Uncle Jim mentioning some older sisters that went to live with another uncle."

"I remember him talking about them, too," replied Ann. "I

12

think there are two sisters, Mary and Susan he said their names were." Then, like a bolt of lightning, Ann's face lit up and she shouted, "Mary! That's the bumpy letter in front of the F on the table. M F, Mary Fielding. Yes, I think this is our house."

After a mini-celebration of their discovery, they were energized and continued looking around the room for more clues as to who lived there. John found a small pile of papers in one corner. There were papers of all different shapes and sizes. One particularly caught his attention. It had a name written across the top under the name of a company. Below the name was a bunch of numbers. He showed it to Ann.

"I don't know what it says," Ann said as she carefully looked over the paper, "But I know this writing across the top are letters and there are numbers written below the letters. I recognize an F in the letters across the top. That might be the start of the word Fielding, but I don't know for sure. Let's keep the paper. I might show it to Uncle Jim when the time is right and he's in a good mood."

They sat down on the mat. After a minute, Ann continued, "You know. We could clean this place up a bit. We could fix it up a little and keep our eyes open for any discarded furniture. Maybe get a chair or two. Nobody is living here. Who would know if we spent some time here? It would be a real house to play house in. How great is that? No other kids are as lucky." When Ann mentioned "other kids," she added some caution, "Don't tell anybody about this place. If we keep it to ourselves, we'll be fine, and we'll have it to ourselves. But as soon as others know about it, we'll lose it. It won't be the same. Uncle Jim will stop us from coming here, or the other kids will tell their parents, and it will cause problems. So, this is just between you and me for now. Let's look upstairs."

On one end of the kitchen was a steep set of stairs leading up to a cramped loft where they could only stand upright in the middle of the room. A few feet on either side of the midst of the room, the roof slant made it impossible for anyone but the shortest people to stand. There were single windows on both ends of the room.

"Let's try to get these windows open to help air it out," Ann said as she walked to one end and tried to release the latch, but with no success. "We need something to hit it with and knock it loose. Maybe a rock will work. Go out and try to find a long, skinny one about the size of your hand."

John raced downstairs and out into the yard energized by the adventure they were having. Then ran back upstairs with the rocks he'd found. Several well-placed hits broke the latch loose, and they could push the window open a few inches before it bound up. But it was enough to allow some air circulation. The only piece of furniture upstairs was a sleeping mat that had become the home of several nests of mice. They walked downstairs, out on the porch and sat down on the front step, glad to be in the fresh air again.

"With sticks and stones, we have conquered our house," Ann announced as though they were the victors in some crusade. Beyond that, she had the unmistakable feeling this was definitely the house they had lived in ten years earlier and now had reclaimed.

CHAPTER

3

"Uncle Jim, don't John and I have some older sisters?" Ann asked a few weeks after they had found the house.

"You sure do, Mary and Susan. A couple of years after your Mum and Pa died, they went to live with Uncle Samuel, my brother. He needed help with his house because his wife was quite sick. Plus, that gave us a little more room in our house.

"Mary Fielding," Ann muttered under her breath remembering the initials carved in the table leg. "That bumpy letter is an M, and I know the next letter was an F," John had heard what she said and was nodding his agreement.

But Uncle Jim was distracted by the knife he was sharpening. "What'd you say, Ann? Speak up. My hearing isn't as good as it used to be."

"Oh, nothing," Ann replied, not wanting to pique his curiosity. A few minutes later when she and John were out of earshot, she continued, "I'm more convinced now than ever. That's our house, the one where we were born. Let's go see it again," as they walked down the road towards what they now considered "their" house.

They were about halfway, passing a pile of rubbish someone had dumped along the road. "Hey, look at that, John," Ann said pointing to a piece of wood sticking out of the pile.

"I just see a piece of wood," replied John.

"Look closer. Come on, let's check it out," Ann shouted as she sprinted in the direction of the rubbish pile. John followed, shaking his head in bewilderment as he wondered what she could see in a pile of garbage that was so exciting. Ann took a step or two up the pile, threw off a rotting animal skin that had been used for a rug, grabbed hold of the wooden piece protruding from the pile and heaved out a chair, or what had been a chair. It was crooked and missing a leg, but to Ann, it was as good as discovering buried treasure. She beamed as she declared, "Our first piece of furniture for our new house."

John rolled his eyes and shook his head. "We can't sit on that. It won't even stand straight on its own, let alone with someone trying to sit on it."

"All it needs is a leg and a little straightening, and it'll be great. We can carve a leg to the right length and tie it in place with this old leather shoelace from this garbage pile."

John mulled over the plan, then with a slight nod added, "That might work. It wouldn't hurt to give it a try." This decision launched their grand effort to furnish their house, which would continue for the next several months.

Uncle Jim became curious and a little concerned when Ann and John would disappear day after day, returning each night just before dark as usual, but exhausted and talking about things such as stools and chairs, knives and forks, pots and pans, wood and coal. "If I didn't know better, it sounds like you two are building a house," Uncle Jim said one evening after supper was over and everyone was settling down for the night.

Ann and John shot each other a serious look. Then Ann gave a slight nod, looked at Uncle Jim and replied, "We've meant to talk to you about something, Uncle Jim."

"You've got my attention," he responded as he worked at reattaching a shoe sole that had started to flap as he walked.

"Remember some months ago I asked you a few questions about where the house was where we were born? Where our house was," Ann added as a way of edging into her next statement. "We found our home, and we've been cleaning it up, fixing it up and finding some furnishings for it." Ann and John were both quiet, watching Uncle Jim closely for how he was receiving this information and how he might react to it.

"Furnishings?" he asked. He could reason through why they would want to find the house and even clean it up after sitting idle for nearly a decade, but finding furnishings indicated someone would want to live there. With his next question, he made a giant leap, "Do you want to live there?" he asked in shock and surprise.

"Eventually," began Ann, then continued before Uncle Jim could respond, "I'll be fourteen in a few months. And when you're fourteen, you can start work in a mill. I've already been asking around, getting information on which mills might be interested. Most fourteen-year-old girls start out as spinsters making thread. I'll have to learn, but I think I could learn quickly. Then, after a few months, if I feel confident in the job, I'd be making steady money. John and I could move into our old place and be on our own."

John was fidgeting fiercely, barely able to stay on his chair, anxious how Uncle Jim might respond. He and Ann had been rehearsing this conversion with Uncle Jim for months. They had gathered up odd pieces of discarded furniture, fixed them up the best they could and put them in the house. They did the same with pots and pans and even spoons, forks and knives. They'd gathered small lumps of coal that had fallen off wagons along the road and had accumulated several hundred pounds by now. They had a small pile of wood made from scraps they'd found and small limbs. The goal of being on their own and self-sufficient was always on their mind. And in the process, they learned they were a team, and as a team, there was little they couldn't eventually accomplish.

"I'll miss having you with us," Uncle Jim said at the end of their conversation. "It sounds like the only thing you'll need is a quilt or two. I think we've got a couple of extra we could send with you, under one condition." Ann and John's ears perked up to hear the condition. "That you not forget us and come by to visit at least once a month."

"Gladly," replied Ann. "And you're always welcome to stop by and see us. We won't be that far away." Then Ann reached into her pocket and pulled out the crumpled paper she and John had found in the house the first day they had discovered it. "We found this in the house, Uncle Jim. Can you tell us what it is?" Ann handed the paper to Uncle Jim. He smoothed it out the best he could, tipped it into several positions trying to find the best light and the best angle to examine it. It was not only faded with age, but much of the writing had become smudged while

18

being carried around for several months in Ann's pocket. He was silent for a long time. Ann noticed a couple of tears rolling down his cheeks. Uncle Jim had become quite a softy as he had grown older.

It took a couple of minutes for him to get his emotions in check before speaking. "This paper brings difficult memories to mind," he said. "This was the last pay chip from the mill where your mum worked before she got so sick. That was the worst year ever for this family, losing both your Pa and Mum in the same year. I kick myself for not doing more to help her. But I was so busy with work and my kids. she was beyond help when I finally realized what was happening. Bringing you kids here to live after she died was the least I could do to honor her memory."

After that evening, John and Ann were more focused than ever on fixing up "their house". Uncle Jim offered his encouragement and advice to the effort.

"We're finding the house has become home to a herd of mice, Uncle Jim," Ann asked a few weeks later. "How's the best way to get rid of them?"

Uncle Jim reached in his pocket, fumbled through several coins, pulled out a Shilling and handed it to Ann. "Go down to the store and buy several rat traps. Clean all the weeds and trash away from the house at least three feet. That bare strip around the house will do as much to keep the mice out of the house as the traps. But you'll have to clear out the ones already in the house. Look closely through the house every few days for the next two weeks to clean the mice out of the traps. If you don't, the house will stink worse than an outhouse from the rotting mice." Then

Uncle Jim got quiet with a big smile on his face. "I'm right proud of you two and what you're doing," he said with glistening eyes. "You're doing it on your own without my help. That coin is the least I could do to help you."

When Ann turned 14, she went to work in a mill saving her money to buy food. Shortly after she started working, John went to work part time for a farmer who sold cheese and eggs to Uncle Jim. Most of his wages were taken as milk, cheese, eggs, corn, barley and occasionally some meat when the farmer butchered a cow, pig or some chickens. He eventually became full time with the farmer. Between both their wages, they could buy the items necessary to keep a household together and even replaced some of their "garbage pile" furniture with some used pieces in good condition.

In a year, they made the official move to their house. They had looked forward to being fully on their own. However, it was an adjustment to learn that all household chores were theirs to do. No other family member, aunt or uncle was going to pick up after them, do the pile of dishes on the table, or keep their clothes washed and mended.

CHAPTER

4

Ann had been spinning for nearly four years on the morning she was late. She had become a competent, dependable and efficient "spinster", as she was known. With no parents, she felt bad she was in such a rush this morning. She knew John needed her company each morning. Being late to work was an annoyance. Ann prided herself on being dependable and on time. It was her reputation. Being late eroded that reputation. She felt being dependable was the most important thing she and her brother had to sell or trade to get what they needed to survive.

She worried the cause of her nausea could have life-altering consequences, and forced the thoughts to the back of her mind. For now, she needed to fix a lunch for John and get to work as soon as possible.

Ann and John lived in a little village about a mile from Oldham called Shaw. On most days, Ann enjoyed the walk, especially in the mornings when the dew had cleaned the air of coal smoke and cotton fibers from the mills running during the day. The air was cool and the other mill workers walking at the same time were content to walk mostly in silence. But today she was late, and the worries that brought with it chased away any enjoyment.

Ann was out of breath as she walked onto the spinning floor, the second floor of the mill. Everyone was already in their places and the rows of spinning wheels were humming, except hers. She quickly moved to her station and smoothly started spinning, hoping to elude the eye of the floor boss, but he had been watching for her. Her floor boss, Joe, had been hired with the mill as a weaver when it opened. But the mill manager soon learned he was better at working with people than with looms. He was friendly and knew enough about the private lives of each of his spinners to exchange small talk about their lives outside the mill, but kept aloof so all the workers understood they kept or lost their jobs on his say so.

A few mills in Oldham were starting to use steam power to drive the spinning and weaving. With steam to supply the power, larger and larger machines were being invented to make more and more cloth. And the world was ready for more cloth. The mill Ann worked in had been built before steam engines were used. The owners were content to let some of the other mills try steam power and see what was involved before they jumped in.[2]

After Ann had been spinning a few minutes, Joe sauntered in her direction. She saw him out of the corner of her eye but tried not to flinch, keeping up the motion of feeding the cotton fibers into the spinning mechanism, hoping he would just walk by.

"I see you were late this morning, Ann," he said in a calm voice, almost with a note of concern.

Ann nodded acknowledgment of the charge. "It won't happen

22

again, Sir," she answered. Ann had learned it didn't matter to Joe what her excuse was, and repeating a litany of excuses or reasons for her tardiness would only exacerbate his annoyance and serve no purpose. He had served notice that he knew she had been late. Both were aware the incident would not be forgotten should he feel she needed discipline if it became too frequent. But right now, he needed every wheel spinning the maximum possible hours. When to fire someone on the spinning floor was completely up to Joe. To Joe, it was all economics. He knew he could find someone else to take her spot within a day or two, but in the meantime, her wheel would sit idle, and he would lose production. Plus, it was always a gamble on how reliable and efficient the new hire would be.

Ann was one of the better spinners. She had been spinning for four years now. Her hands were still nimble and quick and knew the motions needed to make good thread, thread that wouldn't break while in the looms. As a spinner, she was in her prime. Most spinners only lasted into their early 20's. The combination of the cotton fibers in the air and coal smoke eventually drove out many who worked in the mills.

Others married and started families. Or, it would be more accurate to say, they started families then got married. Why be in a hurry to get married and take on the responsibility of a house and wife when the mortality rate for babies of new, young mothers was close to 30%. Real medicine and preventive care were essentially non-existent in that era. Men had the incentive to remain unmarried as long as possible. Not getting married until a healthy baby was a fact, was often the norm. The "family" part is what was bothering Ann this morning. Waking up sick to her stomach on most mornings and being late in the womanly way were sure signs.

There were 32 wheels on this floor, and Ann was one of the best spinners, turning out a pound a day more than the average. To encourage production, each month Joe would announce who the top three producers were. Ann was always in the top three and was often the top producer. So, for now at least, the mental note in both their minds of her tardiness was enough.

CHAPTER

5

On the ground floor of the mill were the looms, twenty looms to be exact. A loom took up more room than a wheel, and they were noisy. It was impossible to speak to anyone while the looms were operating. The banging of the battering bar after each thread was drawn through the weave by the shuttle; the clattering of the shuttle running through the weave; the shifting of the heddles between each shuttle throw and battering; times twenty looms resulted in an extremely noisy, busy floor.

One of the weavers was Joshua. He was the "friend" that had been enjoying Ann's company last night at the pub. And this was not the first evening they had spent in each other's company. Joshua was drawn to Ann the first time he saw her in the lunch shed several months ago. Ann had recently started work at this mill since it was a shorter walk from her home than where she had been working. The lunch shed was not much more than a roof over some tables and benches where the workers, who brought their lunch, ate. Most workers lived close enough to walk home for lunch. For Ann, it was too far to make the round trip and still allow time for lunch and a brief rest before the afternoon work started. Joshua typically didn't bring his lunch and was just walking by the shed on his way home for his meal when he glanced over at those gathering under the roof and noticed Ann. The next day, he brought his lunch.

"Mind if I sit here?" he asked Ann with a faint smile as he indicated he wanted to sit at a place on the opposite side and opposite end of the table, not wanting to appear too forward.

"Sit there if you like," Ann replied, nodding towards the place directly across the table from her.

Joshua picked up on the invitation and moved to the spot across from her, put down his lunch and pulled out the bench. But before sitting down, he put out his hand, looked directly at her and said, "I'm Joshua, Joshua Hardy." His hand hung out towards her in the air for what seemed to him like several minutes.

Ann momentarily froze, surprised by the gesture. It was unusual for a man to offer his hand to a woman. Usually, a man would just tip his hat or nod his head. Joshua realized extending his hand might seem a bit forward. He wanted to indicate he was considering her a coequal, two workers at the same mill.

Ann nearly choking on the bite of food she was chewing as her hand jerked out into his. "I'm Ann," were the only words she could get out of her mouth as she caught her breath looking up directly at him.

"Do you have a last name, Ann?" he said, wanting to help the conversation.

"F-Fielding," Ann squeaked, clearing her throat, taking a quick sip of water, then repeating confidently, "Fielding."

"Nice to meet you, Ann Fielding," he said slowly, warmly, with a hint of a chuckle while continuing to shake her hand. For a few seconds, they looked directly into each other's eyes excluding all distractions around them. What started out as a contrived encounter to meet the new girl, jolted Joshua and reduced his normally smooth, well-practiced introduction, to an awkward attempt at further conversation.

"Sorry… my hands are so rough," he finally stuttered as he sat down. "They're weaver's hands, you know." Ann nodded, Joshua continued, "At least they're not black with coal. I tried working in the mines when I was younger, but being underground all the time got to me. I prefer seeing the sun when it shines. Some people prefer being underground. The weather doesn't matter down there; it's always the same."

"How long ago did you work in the mines?" she asked to continue the conversation.

"Let's see," Joshua was glad for the question since it gave him the opportunity to summarize his life in answer to her question. "I started in the mines as a door tender at 11, moved up to thruster at 12, after four years moved to loader for four years, and then swung a pick for three years. That's when I'd had enough of the mine and got a job at another mill as a freight mover for five years. I always wanted to move up to weaver, better pay you know. I kept my eyes open for a mill that would train me. When a position opened here about two years ago, I came to this mill."

"I know there are a lot of coal mines nearby, and I should know more about coal mining than I do," Ann responded. "My father was a miner but was killed in an accident when I was quite young. I knew very little of him. What do those different positions do?" Ann was enjoying the company and conversation almost as much as Joshua was explaining about his experience.

"A door tender takes no skill, other than staying awake and being aware when a cart is coming down the track. To keep enough air circulating to the miners, you must keep the doors closed so the air is directed down the shaft and doesn't escape. But when a cart comes, you need to open the door so the cart can go through without stopping. Then close the door right after the cart. A thruster is one who pushes the cart from where it's loaded to where it's dumped. This job doesn't take any brains, but it's one of the hardest, most grueling jobs in a mine. And something as simple as stopping for a door that's not open is a significant waste of time and energy. It takes a lot of effort to stop or start a loaded cart. A loader shovels coal into the carts and a picker swings a pick ax all day, breaking chunks of coal from the vein. Now you're an expert in coal mining," Joshua joked, trying to keep the conversation moving.

"Did you grow up in Oldham?" Ann asked.

"I grew up near Bradford, in a little village next to Bradford called Wibsey." Joshua could see Ann was trying to place where Bradford was, so he added, "It's about 25 miles northeast of here" as he pointed in a generally northeast direction. He continued, "When there are nine children in the family, space and food are tight, so you move out when you're quite young. But we get together quite often."

"Are your parents still living?" Ann asked, being a bit forward. But they both seemed comfortable getting to know each other and Joshua was quite willing to share information.

"Yes, they are. But Pa is doing quite poorly having worked in the mines most of his life. He has a terrible time breathing and especially sleeping. So does everyone else in the house with his coughing through the night."

"I'm sorry to hear that," replied Ann. "With all the cotton in the air around here, I'm not sure working here is much better than a coal mine."

"I'm doing all the talking. Tell me about you, Ann." Just then the back-to-work whistle blew, and lunch was over.

"Maybe tomorrow," Ann replied as she gathered her sack and wrappings, hoping this pleasant conversation would indeed continue the next day. As she walked back to her wheel, she felt quite pleased and excited at her new acquaintance. His comment about being a coal miner when he was "younger" got her wondering just how old he was. She thought of him again sitting across the table, with more scrutiny, through a critical eye. She remembered a few stands of grey in his sideburns. And his eyes, when she first looked into his eyes, she was transfixed. They were such kind eyes. But now she remembers, the kind appearance was enhanced by faint lines at the corners. *"Yes, he is older, much older, maybe ten years older than me,"* she said to herself. Even though Joshua was no longer living at his family home, she envied the fact that both his parents were still alive and that he had so many others to help support the family.

After settling into the familiar routine of spinning thread, her mind shifted into auto-pilot, and she started adding up the years in Joshua's jobs to determine just how old he was. It took a while since she lost her place and had to start over a few times. Then she lost count again when she had to reach over to pull closer part of the fluffy cotton mound the carders had piled between her and the next wheel. But when she made it all the way through her addition, her free hand flew to her mouth briefly. "It can't be," she thought to herself. She started through the additions again. "*I can't believe it. He's 34!*" she muttered to herself, her thoughts becoming lost in the whine of the wheels spinning in the room. In amazement, she muttered aloud, "He's 17 years older than me! Nearly twice my age!"[3]

CHAPTER
6

The walk home that afternoon was a welcome chance to mull over the events of the day in quiet. As she walked, she was having quite a conversation with herself. *"I can't believe how old he is,"* was the main reoccurring thought. *"And his manner was quite cordial and respectful, not like most men my age. Most are married and had a family by his age. Maybe he is married. We didn't talk about that. I need to find out next time we meet. Maybe we won't meet again; maybe he'll go home for lunch and not bring his lunch tomorrow. I guess that would settle it."*

There was no question Ann was drawn to her new acquaintance, but now she had a mental fork in her thoughts. If Joshua was married, then she must assume he was just being cordial to a fellow mill worker. On the other hand, if he was not married, he may be looking to develop a relationship. Her conversation with herself continued, *"But why would he not be married? He's nice looking enough, polite, confident, speaks well and seems well settled. After all, according to him, he's been working for over 20 years now."* Again, she was shocked to realize he had been working longer than she had been alive. Her thoughts continued, *"He did mention his father was not well. His father probably had to retire from the mines early due to ill health and he and his brothers work to support his parents."* As Ann rounded the last corner before reaching home, John who was out in the yard, noticed her and came out to meet her.

"I watched a calf being born today," John excitedly told her. After reciting, what he deemed were the pertinent details of the event, he asked, "How was your day? Did you get in trouble for being late?"

"No. No trouble, but Joe, the floor boss, did mention it to me. I need to be sure it doesn't happen again." Then Ann couldn't help saying, "I did eat lunch with a nice man from the loom floor. His name is Joshua." She tried hard to be as deadpan and indifferent as possible, but John picked up on a note of excitement in her voice. His first instinct was to immediately resent the incursion by this other man into their world, the world the two of them had created and worked hard for. The previous few years had been extremely hard as they worked together to establish a home and hold it together as a family. Now, with Ann having steady work at the mill and John working full time with the farmer, they were getting by without the constant possibility of it falling apart. They felt more secure than ever before.

They walked to the house in silence. Ann interpreted Johns silence as resentment for Joshua, and she kicked herself for even mentioning it. John remained silent until they turned into the yard. Then he softened and realized this might be a good thing. "Is he from around here?" he asked to get passed the silence.

"He lives in Oldham now, but he's from Bradford, or more accurately, Wibsey, a little village about 25 miles northeast of here." Ann sat in a chair on the porch to enjoy the evening before going in the house. John went into the house and came out nibbling on a big chunk of cheese, broke it in two, handed some to Ann and sat down to continue the conversation.

"Tell me about the calf today," Ann said to John.

He recounted a few details then paused a few seconds, giving due consideration and respect for the birthing cow. Now, that being old news, he continued. "Tell me about Joshua."

Ann was embarrassed that mention of her lunch conversation had stuck in his mind. She was now self-conscious that the conversation was revolving around what was meant to be, no more than a casual remark about the happenings of the day. But at the same time, she felt excited, even a bit giddy. "It was nothing. He happened to sit at the same table I was at in the lunch shed, and we talked during lunch," Ann tried to minimize the event.

John straightened in his chair for a few seconds, cleared his throat then relaxed again and continued gnawing on his fist full of cheese. "Go on," prodded John.

Now the dam broke, the wall breached, and nearly every word that had been spoken at lunch was repeated sitting on the porch, eating cheese in the setting sun. Ann finished with, "He usually goes home to eat lunch. He only lives a block away from the mill. We'll see if he brings his lunch tomorrow."

The next day Ann sat in her usual spot and tried to look bored and detached as she pawed through the bread, cheese and a little pork she had brought from home. Her outer appearance may be deceiving others who had gathered in the shed, but her inner thoughts were a rapid-fire barrage of questions, answers, pleas, and wishes. Twice she convinced herself yesterday was a one-time occurrence and Joshua was onto other interests. Then she reminded herself it had only been five minutes since the lunch whistle blew and it often took weavers a few extra minutes if they were setting a new bolt of cloth or changing the mix of weft and warp.

Ann choked and coughed a little when he suddenly showed up at her table smiling big, big enough that Ann thought, "*He must be enjoying this. That's a good sign.*"

"Sorry, it took me some extra time. I had to change the heddle set up," Joshua said smoothly as he sat across from her.

"I can recite spinning methods and detailed until you're bored to sleep. But I know little about weaving," Ann said.

"In weaving, the weft is the threads that run side to side, put in place by the shuttle running back and forth. The warp is the threads that run lengthwise. The heddles raise some threads allowing the shuttle to pass over or under certain threads. Pressing a different heddle will raise different threads allowing for different patterns and thread mixture to be woven into the cloth. But you probably already knew all that. I've been anxious to hear about you and your family," he said as he settled in to absorb everything Ann was about to say, apple in one hand and a chunk of some meat in the other.

Except for a few questions, Joshua listened quietly, eating his lunch. Ann explained she lived about a mile from the mill with her brother in the family home. She also told a little about where John worked and her parents both passing away before she and John were old enough to remember. When she explained that her

34

parents had passed, she thought it would be a good time to ask the question preying on her mind. With all her concentration, she tried to sound as ambivalent as possible when she asked, "Do you have a wife, kids?" She looked away from him across the yard while she spoke so he wouldn't see the intense interest she had in the question.

Joshua looked directly at her, smiled and was content to wait and wait until she couldn't stand it anymore and looked back at him for his answer. "I'm not married. I've never been married." He said. "And I know your next question. Why not? Two reasons. With Pa being so sick, any money I don't need to live on goes back to him and Mum. He continues to get worse, and I don't expect he'll live much longer. The second reason is I haven't found the right woman," he paused then added, "until now."

Before long they were spending part of every weekend and several late nights each week in each other's company. Ann could tell John had mixed feelings about the budding relationship.

"I've asked Joshua to join us for Sunday dinner," Ann said to John. She felt John resented her for being gone from home so much. That left more of the cooking, cleaning, and washing to him. She thought this may be a way for John to get to know Joshua and defuse his resentment. "He makes me so happy, happier than I'have been since, well, since ever. The fret and worry that always seemed to hang over my head has evaporated. Joshua seems to give me strength and optimism for the future. We've became close, very close, eating lunch every day together. Even when the conversation lags, just being around each other feels good."

John was quiet, considering what Ann had just told him. He finally nodded and said, "I can't recall a time when you've been so happy. I'll see if I can bring home a chicken from the farm to roast."

CHAPTER

7

Ann could no longer ignore the fact she was pregnant. Her life was about to take a sharp turn, regardless of what happened with Joshua. On one hand, Ann was excited about having a baby, a child of her own, her family. But how would Joshua react? That was the key to whether her life would be better or worse a year from now. When with Joshua, Ann tried to mask her worry and questions and tried to delay the inevitable conversation that would re-color this relationship that had been so pleasant, reassuring and fun.

Being unmarried and pregnant was not rare. Ann knew of two others on her spinning floor who were pregnant and not married. Being women mostly in their teens and early twenties, it was always on their minds and occasionally a topic of discussion in the lunch shed and at the pub. For the men, it was nearly always a topic of discussion when any of them were together.

Among the women, it was generally not considered a sign of promiscuity if the women had a steady boyfriend. Otherwise, if they felt you were sleeping around, the pregnant woman was shunned, generally sitting alone in the lunch shed and not included in groups chatting before or after work. Before she met Joshua, Ann rarely went out at night. She felt the responsibility of being head of her household and took little time for herself.

Joshua changed that. It wasn't long until one night while sharing a few drinks at the pub, Joshua noticed that Ann was unusually sullen, and had been for several weeks now. Ann tried to pass it off as just a hard day at work, but couldn't persuade Joshua. Finally, Ann realized she couldn't put it off any longer. She took a deep breath, looked up at Joshua and mentally commented to herself, "Here it goes."

Ann stated with as steady a voice as she could muster, "Joshua, I'm pregnant." Joshua looked briefly into her eyes to verify she wasn't just joking around. Then he looked away, into an empty corner of the room, then looked down into his drink. He was silent. Ann knew this would hit him hard. He would need a few minutes to absorb this information before responding. She allowed him time to consider this news and kept quiet. All the good times they had enjoyed for months now could be wiped away in a moment or reinforced, depending on his response.

Of course, Ann's hope was that he would want to marry her. She would marry him tonight if he asked. She also realized being a bachelor had become ingrained into who he was, especially at his age. The longer his silence persisted, the less likely his response would be positive. Still, she allowed him the courtesy of taking as much time as he wanted.

When he spoke, his response was weak and unsteady, communicating just the opposite of the words that came out of his mouth, "That's great. But my father is not well, and I have to..."

That was all Ann needed to hear. In that instant, her hope for building a life with Joshua exploded into tiny pieces. She staggered out of the room as if she had been hit with a bale of cotton, leaving Joshua in mid-sentence. As she left, a man sitting near the door was puzzled to hear her say, "That's great, but…" Then she repeated in anger and a derogatory tone, "That's great, BUT!!" She headed towards home. Not knowing which was moving faster, her feet on the road or her thoughts and words coming from her mouth. "I guess I've found out what kind of a man Joshua Hardy is. I see now why he's not married. Who would want such a spineless snake for a husband?" Ann even surprised herself at how vicious she felt right now and felt no regret for her anger. "Have a drink, have fun, get cozy with a gal, then when things get complicated, move on to the next one," she raved on as a summary and epitaph to their relationship. She blindly put one foot in front of the other on the familiar path, not caring about the strange looks she was getting as she passed the late evening travelers.

John had been in bed about 20 minutes when he heard her come in the front door, making an unusual amount of noise. "This is not good," he said to himself as he now listened closely for more clues to Ann's frame of mind. John could hear she went straight to her room and shut the door, not slamming it, but not quietly either. The amount of noise she was making was unusual. It was hours earlier than she usually came home when she was with Joshua. John was now wide awake and continued to lay still listening for more clues to Ann's frame of mind. A few minutes later, he heard her sobbing in her room. He felt sorry for her. He didn't need to know details but suspected that in the morning, the happy, energetic Ann would no longer exist and would be replaced with the exacting, head-of-the-household, get your chores done "parent" she was before meeting Joshua.

In the pub, Joshua sat frozen in his chair. He felt terrible and even surprised himself at how bad he felt. He thought this day might come, as familiar as they had been with each other. But he was always able to put off thinking through what he would do when this day came. So now when he faced Ann, he was not prepared. He realized his response was weak and sloppy. It was not at all how he felt. His opinion of himself took a nosedive. "Maybe she's better off without me," he thought to himself. Then realized he was only trying to put some salve on the wound he had inflicted on himself. Seeing he was drinking alone, a couple of guys came up and tried to buddy up to him. "Not tonight guys," he said staring straight ahead. The two men got the message and slithered off.

Joshua questioned himself, "*How do I feel?*" He knew how he responded was not how he felt. But how did he feel? He was in new territory. He felt differently about Ann than he had felt about anyone before, ever. But how did he feel? The question rolled through his mind every few seconds. He needed answers only he could supply. *"Am I ready to give up being a bachelor and settle into being a husband, a family man, and provider?"* That last word, provider, scared him. He recoiled when he thought about it. He was OK with being a husband. He could get used to the idea of being a family man. But provider? To have a family dependent on him for food, clothes and a home was a new concept for him. He had been helping support his parents for several years now, but there were eight others in the family to help shoulder that burden. The whole burden didn't fall to him.

Even if he accepted the responsibility, married Ann, and accepted being the father of their child, the damage had been done, severe damage. He knew it and felt rotten about it. *"Can it be repaired, ever?"* he muttered to himself. A vivid recollection burst into his mind of a time he was visiting his parents a little over a year earlier.

He and three of his brothers were visiting with their father while he lay on his bed. The father sensed his time was growing short. Between coughing spells, he managed to get out this statement, "Sometime in your lives you'll realize that one of the few things that really matter is how you've treated other people. You can say you're sorry for something you've said, but you can never erase the words first heard." What else he might have said about it was obliterated by another coughing fit. The statement "You can never really erase the words heard," was burning a hole in Joshua tonight.

Several hours later and several, several drinks later he was kicked out of the pub as the proprietor locked the door behind him. He staggered home and passed out crosswise on the bed, fully dressed, including shoes and hat.

CHAPTER

8

Ann slept little through the night, not wanting to accept the harsh reality she faced a life of motherhood as a single person. Her storybook dream of a husband, home and family were nonexistent now. As John expected, she was sharp and direct, but measured in her communications with him. "Don't take your stupidity out on him," she muttered to herself as she went about her morning duties.

They left the house about the same time, Ann to the mill and John to the farm. Ann hadn't said anything about the night before, and John didn't ask.

"I guess she and Joshua broke up," John said softly to no one. He was glad for this chance to think through what appeared to be a dramatic change in circumstances. "I'd better not ask her anything about Joshua for the next while unless she brings it up. I can tell she's mad about something. I best be careful if I don't want to feel the brunt of her anger."

Joshua spent the night in liquor induced sleep but woke up in physical pain. When he tried to remember why he hurt so much, it threw him into mental pain as well, disgusted at the way he had handled the situation. It was getting light outside, so pain or no pain, he forced himself to get upright, grab some food and head out the door.

That day at lunch, Ann still sat in the lunch shed but moved to a corner away from her usual spot. It was easier to deal with the painful events of the previous 24 hours by changing her surroundings even a small amount. Staring at the meager amount of food she brought, she quickly finished her lunch and left the shed, opting to leave the factory property for a short walk around the block. Still seething, she avoided conversation with anyone before the afternoon shift.

By lunch time, Joshua was finally starting to feel some relief from the massive amount of alcohol he had consumed the night before. What small physical relief he felt was pushed aside by the stark realization of his inability to face this situation honestly, while hurting and betraying Ann in the process. The pain was magnified, realizing he cared for her more deeply than any other person who had been part of his life. But what could he do now? He stayed away from the shed as he walked home for his lunch but walked close enough to glance at the chair where she always sat. Seeing it empty, he mentally kicked himself again. He realized she had become much more than a good friend. The damage was severe; he feared unsalvageable. He had lost someone whom he cared for deeply, and it hurt.

Days passed which turned into weeks with no interaction between them. But there wasn't a day that Joshua didn't spend a significant part of the day rolling three questions over in his mind, *"What can I do now? What should I do now? Am I ready to become a husband, father, and provider?"* The "provider" part of the last questions always got stuck in his mind and sent him off on a self-evaluation of himself, his abilities, and his ongoing responsibilities he felt to his parents. It was showing in his work. Twice in one day, he lost track of the weave pattern and had to stop the loom, cut and pull out the previous half dozen shuttle threads, and knot the shuttle thread to proceed again. The thread would occasionally break in the normal course of weaving and would cause delays. That was a given.

The first time the floor boss noticed Joshua pulling out several of the previous threads, he knew it was not a broken thread and made a mental note. The second time it happened, he walked by Joshua. "That's twice in the last hour, Joshua. Is something the matter?" he said.

"No, sir. I just lost my focus. I'll do better." Joshua nervously replied. He was surprised at how his feelings for Ann were unrelenting, even after a couple of months since their break-up. Loom operators were trained to knot a broken thread in such a way as to be only noticeable under scrutiny by a trained eye. But a mistake in the weave pattern, if not corrected, would send a whole bolt of cloth to the "discard" bin and was often sold for less than half price. "While at work, I've got to concentrate on work and not think of Ann. I'll have plenty of time after work to think about it," he argued with himself. The fact that she was just one floor above him didn't help. He caught himself looking up at the ceiling, estimating the position of her wheel on the floor above, and realized, all this time, she was less than 20 feet away through the ceiling on the floor above.

Joshua's thinking was slowly entering new territory. A couple of times while at his loom, he imagined going home after work, not to a couple of housemates, but to a loving wife and child and a hot cooked meal, spending the evening enjoying each other's company. *"I've got to keep my weave right,"* he chided himself. "Just one more mental look at that warm home with Ann and the baby." But he was jolted when the mental picture included something he hadn't seen before, several children.

One floor up at precisely the spot Joshua had calculated, Ann was quietly spinning, having made peace gradually with the reality that she was going to be a single parent. Conditioned to plan ahead since her parents died, she had thought long and hard about how their lives, she and her brother's, would play out in the coming months and years ahead. She hadn't said anything to John yet about the baby, but couldn't put it off much longer. She was beginning to show and put on some weight. She even caught Joe, the floor boss, eyeing her over several times in the last few days. He didn't say anything, but the look on his face said, *"What's going on here?"* It would only be a few days, and he'd be asking her the very personal question, "Are you pregnant, Ann?"

She wouldn't deny it but knew she best have a plan already in place if she didn't want him replacing her right away. She'd keep working as long as she could make the walk back and forth between home and the mill, hopefully to within a few days of the birth. When the baby came, she would have to take 2 – 3 weeks off to recuperate and get the baby off to a good start. Being absent from work for 2-3 weeks was risky. If Ann didn't make arrangement for a substitute, Joe would bring in someone else so her wheel wasn't idle. *"I'll have to be better than anyone who might be brought in so Joe will be anxious to have me back,"* she thought. Spinsters getting pregnant and leaving work was not uncommon. Some never came back due to long term health problems caused by the pregnancy and birth. Some found other ways to replace the money brought in. Since Ann was the main source of income in her household, there was never any question about coming back.

The changes that were upcoming were daunting. *"I wish I could talk to Jenny. She'd have some good advice,"* she thought. Jenny was a spinner when Ann started at this mill. She had been a spinner a long time, had never married, and was a good example of why the word "spinster" became associated with older, unmarried women. Jenny and Ann hit it off and became good friends. They spent most lunch hours and a few evenings talking as Jenny saw Ann as one who could use, and who would appreciate, her years of various experiences. Ann, being without parents, was hungry for just the kind of things Jenny had to say, except when it came to men. In that area, Jenny had little experience, nor much interest in getting any. And that was just the area Ann could have used some good, rigid advice. It might have kept her out of the situation she now found herself. Jenny had retired a few months ago after years of spinning cotton. *"Maybe Jenny would fill in for me while I have the baby,"* Ann thought. *"I know she has no interest in continuing to work, so she would not be a threat to my job. Joe liked her, so he should have no problem with having her back for a while. And when I'm able to come back to work, maybe Jenny would tend the baby for a while until I figure out something else."*

Ann liked her plan. It took a difficult situation and turned it to the best possible outcome. *"The only thing that would make it better is for me to have a husband and for this baby to have a father."* She cringed as this thought ran through her mind. She stuffed it in the back of her brain somewhere and instead thought, *"The next step is to discuss this with John. I'll do it this coming Sunday.*

We'll be home all day and will have unhurried time to talk through it. If it goes well, I'll then talk to Jenny."

CHAPTER

9

Sunday rolled around before Ann knew it. She had rehearsed several scenarios as to just how she would tell John. She had caught John looking at her with a question on his face but declined to elaborate further.

After they finished eating breakfast on Sunday morning, they were talking about what had happened the previous week and what they expected to occur in the coming week. This morning, Ann was anxious to discuss what she had on her mind. "I have something to tell you," she said as John finished the last of his fried eggs. With wide eyes, he went on high alert. Ann continued, "Joshua and I broke up a couple of months ago."

"I assumed that when you quit going out at night," shrugged John. "Is that it?" he questioned.

"No," then after a long pause and a deep breath, she continued, "I'm pregnant." This last bombshell not only shocked John but didn't seem to go with her first statement about breaking up with Joshua. Ann let him stew in his confusion for a short time, then continued. "When I told Joshua about the baby, he wanted nothing to do with me."

Incredulous, John blurted out, "Did he say that?"

"Not exactly. But he immediately started making excuses about having to support his parents, and he is busy, and he had soup for dinner the night before, so he wasn't interested in being the father of his baby." John rolled his eyes and wrinkled up his forehead, squinting as if that would help make sense of her last comment about 'having soup for dinner.' Seeing his muddle, Ann continued, "What I'm saying, it doesn't matter what lame excuse you use; the question is simply 'Are you going to be a man about this or not?'" John was nodding as her meaning became clear. She stood up, looked John straight in the eye and said in the most absolute tone she could muster, "I'm telling you right now John, as plainly as I can, if you ever put a girl in the same condition I'm in, you'd better be prepared to be a man about it, or I'll disown you as my brother." Ann sat back down to catch her breath. The previous few minutes had taken a lot out of her. She was also relieved. She could now share with others the burden she had kept to herself.

John interrupted the silence, "So, you're going to have a baby?" he asked carefully, getting back to the point of the conversation before it took a detour around Joshua.

"Yes," replied Ann, "and with Joshua out of the picture, here's what we'll do." She then repeated the plans she had been mulling over now for weeks, including talking to Jenny about substituting for her at the mill when the baby was born. John was supportive and even a little excited at the prospects of an infant in their home.

A week later, Ann went to see Jenny. Jenny opened the door a crack to see who was knocking at her door on a Sunday morning. When she saw Ann, she immediately threw open the door and with outstretched arms screamed, "Ann! It's so good to see you," then grabbed her in a big bear hug. But she immediately backed away, eying Ann carefully up and down and said, "What's going on here?" as she realized there was more to Ann than the petite, slender girl she expected to see.

"I have some news I've come to share with you," Ann said, trying to sound upbeat. But her upbeat tone of voice trailed off as she ran out of optimism and the sentence ended with a whimper.

"Come in and let's talk. I'll get us some tea," Jenny said. She guided Ann to the table and chairs in her kitchen. Jenny was as close to a mother figure as anyone could be in Ann's life. With Jenny, she could relate all the worry and frustration of the previous months and Jenny would sit quietly with few questions and take it all in. Ann was surprised at how much she had been holding inside. Much of what Ann said, she hadn't even shared with John, wanting to shield him from as much of the pain and worry as she could.

"It's a shame it didn't work out with Joshua," Jenny finally said. There was more than an hour of history from the first meeting in the lunch shed to the breakup at the pub. "You're in territory I've never been in. I haven't had many suitors. The few I have had, I have discouraged, even been ornery to them. I was always afraid of what has happened to you. I would never let myself get close to a fella for fear I would get hurt. I guess that makes me a bit of a coward. Now I'm getting up in years, alone, that hurts as well. I've come to realize that you can't avoid getting hurt. All you can do is affect the timing."

"But getting back to you. Of course, I'll fill in at the mill for you. I think I would enjoy being back with the crew for a time. Knowing it is temporary would even make it more enjoyable. Taking care of the baby for a while after it's born would be a treat. I've not had any of my own, of course, but have tended several nieces and nephews over the years. I think I can remember how it's done. One more thing, don't write off Joshua completely. Leave the door open a crack. He hasn't acted too smart up to this point, but this may just be the thing to make a man out of him. He's getting older along with the rest of us. Some of us take more years than others to grow up."

The visit with Jenny was a big bandage on the sore that had been festering in Ann's soul. John could see a marked difference after she returned. She was more cheerful, confident and enjoyable to be around.

Jenny's comment about 'leaving the door open a crack' got Ann to thinking. *"I have slammed that door closed and shut Joshua out,"* Ann thought to herself at work the next day as she mindlessly performed the methodical hand-dance of feeding cotton fibers into the spinning wheel. *"How could I test his attitude and determine his feelings without opening myself up to more pain and rejection?"*

For the next several weeks, Ann thought through several ideas on how she might determine what Joshua's state of mind was. She thought of sending John to his home with some message. She thought of having her floor boss, or his floor boss, run into him while at the pub and ask him about her. But each of these scenarios involved a third person that may allow the whole situation to get out of control, out of her control.

She settled on a plan where she would approach him herself. She wasn't scared of him, but she was afraid her anger might get out of control. She might say things to make it worse, not better. She had to work on this before the encounter. "I'm as much at fault as he is for being pregnant," she thought. "He didn't force me into this situation. If I refused him, I was afraid he would cut me off, and I'd lose him," she admitted. These were thoughts she hadn't allowed herself to have before. "As it turned out, I lost him anyway. That wasn't too smart, either." Taking responsibility for her condition was a new line of thinking. It took several days for her to come to terms with this new mind-set.

It was dusk as the work shift was ending for the day. The sun dictated how much work was accomplished since lighting provided by open flame would be very dangerous in a mill. It was well into fall and the days were getting shorter. It had rained earlier, so the air was fresh and clean. The many spring and fall rains had the benefit of air cleaned of cotton fibers and coal smoke, which were suffocating at other times.

Ann hurried from her spinning wheel down the stairs and outside hoping to be there before Joshua left for the day. She stood off to the side where she had a good view of the workers as they left. Joshua walked through the door wiping the sweat and grime off his face, sucking in a couple of deep breaths of the clean, cooler air. He stared at the ground in front of him as he walked and didn't notice Ann walking up to his side. "Joshua, can I speak to you for a minute," she asked, indicating she wanted him to follow her away from the oncoming crowd exiting the building.

"Of course," replied a surprised Joshua, looking Ann over

carefully and noticing she was about seven months into the pregnancy. He'd been hoping for some interaction for months. Now she had surprised him and he had no words but followed her blindly a few yards to be away from the crowd and out of earshot.

"I want to say I feel terrible how we, I mean, I left things. I've made arrangements for a midwife, and for Jenny to fill in for me here at the mill when I have our baby." Then, before he could respond, she spun around and melted into the very crowd of people she was avoiding seconds before.

Joshua kept repeating over and over the two sentences she had uttered. An ache grew inside. *"Why didn't I say something? What would I have said? She didn't give me a chance to say anything and has arranged for a fill-in while she has our baby?"* Our baby, our baby." He couldn't quit repeating those last two words, which were reinforced by the sight of her rounded belly. For the past several weeks now, Ann had to change how she sat at her wheel. She could no longer sit up close, directly facing it. She had to do her spinning "side saddle" to get close enough to feed the cotton fibers onto the spindle.

As he walked home, for the rest of the evening, and for several days after he analyzed from every angle the two sentences Ann had spoken. *"She didn't ask me to do anything. There was no request for support of any kind. She didn't say she blamed me. She did say she felt bad about the way she left things, even though I'm to blame for how poorly this was handled."* He was impressed with her mature, non-condescending approach. He found his feelings for her growing even stronger.

54

CHAPTER

10

66 John, come here!" The call carried an urgency John had not heard before. Ann was feeling pain she had not felt before. John hurried down the stairs and into the bedroom where Ann slept. "It's time. I'm sure this is it." Just then, another contraction hit Ann with an intensity that surprised her, and she cried out. "Get the midwife. Then go to Jenny's and ask her to start at the mill tomorrow." John, on the verge of hyperventilating, headed out the door.

Ann had begun feeling sick yesterday walking home from work, flu-like and achy. She thought she had a couple more weeks before the delivery was due, but after arriving home she started thinking about having Jenny start for her at the mill. "I'll give it one more day. If I don't feel better, I'll have her start." She continued to feel depressed and full of aches. About midnight the pains started. They came about every 20 minutes, then got closer and more intense. Now, it was four o'clock in the morning and still dark outside, but there was no question the baby was coming.

Thirty minutes later the mid-wife arrived, a mature woman, well wrinkled with massive arms and legs. She went about the business of preparing the bed for the birthing of a child. She boosted Ann into the best position and hardly strained when she lifted her off the mat with one hand to place additional towels under her, anticipating what normally accompanies a childbirth. Then she prepared a mat with a blanket for the baby. When all appeared ready, she sat down to rest and wait. Between pains, Ann asked, "How many babies have you delivered?"

"I quit counting several years ago when I passed four hundred," She said with a slight smile. "You'll be fine. Things are moving along quite well. Here, drink this. It will take the edge off the pain. It may slow the birth down a little, but most women will take the trade-off." She handed Ann a cup containing a milky liquid.

"What is it?" asked Ann.

"Laudanum. It's best to use it sparingly. Take a little now, and if it gets intolerable, I'll give you a little more. If I give you too much, you'll sleep through the birth, but it won't be over until tomorrow." She said this as one who had seen women in every condition.

Ann stared at the liquid, debating whether to drink it. The onset of the most severe pain made up her mind for her. The cup was empty in one swallow.

About this time, John arrived back home. He stood briefly at the door to the room and reported all was set with Jenny. He was undecided as to stay in the room or leave. He had an interest in seeing the birth of Ann's baby but felt extremely awkward at seeing his sister in this condition. As soon as the next contraction he saw Ann roll her eyes in pain. He slipped out the front door closing it tightly behind him and started walking down the street out of earshot.

Joshua was clearly aware the delivery day was fast approaching. He made a point to notice Ann's arrival and how she looked each morning while carefully avoiding any interaction. He wanted to be involved, but also realized it was no longer up to him. The brief and concise meeting Ann engineered a couple of months earlier was a clear message she was determined to see this through on her own. But at the same time, her regret at "how things ended" told him she would like to have him as part of the family if he was ready to make the necessary, total commitment. He wasn't ready yet and wondered if he ever would be.

When Ann failed to show up to work this morning, and he noticed Jenny was there to take her place, he couldn't help but approach her. "Is Ann having our baby?" he blurted out as she entered the mill.

"Our baby?" Jenny looked directly into his eyes and without any hesitation launched into him. "I see. You're the one who put her in this condition. How can you claim even a speck of ownership when you scamper off with your tail between your legs and go on enjoying life?"

Joshua took a step back, eyes wide and mouth stuck half open as if he wanted to say something, needed to say something, but could produce no words. He was tempted to walk away, but he couldn't argue with what Jenny was saying, and he didn't know yet if Ann was in labor. "A man, a real man, would be right with her while she experiences some of the worst pain she'll have in her life," Jenny continued nearly shouting. "But maybe you've already given her that pain when you got her pregnant About this time, John arrived back home. He stood briefly then refused any responsibility." The other workers, seeing the ongoing conflict, walked as far away as possible. Jenny slowly backed away, keeping an unflinching stare into Joshua's eyes until she started up the stairs to the second floor. The verbal slap in the face stunned him. He stood motionless for several minutes realizing he deserved the most severe rebuke he'd ever received.

Ann was on the verge of asking for more laudanum, slipping

in and out of conscience thought as the pains came and left. In a moment of clearness, she thought, "It's time this baby was born." At the next contraction, she bore down with all remaining strength.

The midwife, watching carefully remarked, "That was real good, Ann. One more like that and we'll have a baby."

The comment gave Ann hope that the end of this ordeal may be close. As the next contraction started, she knew she had little more to give but determined to push as best she could. Thankfully, it was enough.

"You have a beautiful baby boy," remarked the midwife as she cut the cord. "I'll clean him up, and you can hold him."

Ann closed her eyes and drifted off to relish some much-needed rest from the previous 10 hours. It seemed like only seconds until the midwife was handing Ann the new, tightly bundled baby boy. As she looked for the first time at her new son, the name "James" came strongly to her. She quietly muttered, "James." Followed by, "James Fielding," Followed by, "James Hardy Fielding," she said resolutely. There was no question the father should be involved. In that instant, Ann determined she would work to include Joshua as part of this family.

Word of James' birth spread quickly through the mill. Joshua was still reeling from his encounter with Jenny, not anxious for any opportunity for a repeat. He did enjoy the notoriety and celebrated by buying drinks for the mill workers at the pub. As his buddies left the pub and the noise died down, Joshua was left in relative quiet to think about his newborn son. He ached to hold him and look at him. He longed to be in the room with his son and Ann, sharing the first precious minutes of James' life. He longed to be the father he had been avoiding. He determined to make it happen.

CHAPTER

11

"John, would you see who is at the door? I'm in the middle of bathing James," Ann shouted to John. It was mid-morning, on a Sunday. James was six weeks old and was growing and getting stronger. Ann had reluctantly returned to work. She looked forward to Sunday, to be able to spend the whole day with James, marveling at the progress he had made the previous week. She had little time to spend with him during the week, leaving early for work and returning late. Jenny was thoroughly enjoying James during the day while Ann was away.

"Can I help...," Johns sentence trailed off as he opened the door and realized who was standing in front of him -- Joshua.

"I came to see Ann and the baby," Joshua said apologetically, John's mouth still open in surprise.

"Wait here," John shut and latched the door as he scurried to where Ann was playing with James in a tub of water. "It's Joshua," is all he said to Ann.

Ann's eyes grew wide in surprise, but she took her time in thinking about the situation, both to prepare herself mentally for the encounter and to purposely make Joshua wait outside the door, stewing in a mixture of built up anxiety and humility.

Indeed, Ann had accomplished much in the last few years without his help whatsoever. Not only preparing for and having a child, but finding this house and making it, with John's help, their home. It was quite an accomplishment for two teenagers.

But Ann wanted and needed Joshua's help, which would be a big step. "Now is a good time. He can help me bathe James. Invite him in," Ann casually replied.

"Ann says you can come in. She bathing James right now," John said as he opened the door wide for Joshua. Everyone was on edge at this first encounter after James' birth. Each one in the room had their mixture of thoughts, feelings, and perceptions. Each one was sensitive to what was said, how each moved and showed regard to the others. Everyone wanted a positive outcome, but no one had a clear picture as to how that might happen.

"Hello, Joshua," Ann said in a calm, confident tone. Joshua said nothing, just nodding his acknowledgment of Ann's greeting. "James, your Pa has come to see you," Ann said as she rinsed the remaining soap. "Joshua, would you hand me that towel?" Ann asked pointing to a towel she had laid out on the table before the bath began. She lifted James out of the water, wrapped the towel around him, then handed him to Joshua. "James, meet your daddy." Joshua, bewildered by the gesture, clumsily took James, holding him tightly with both arms, clearly rattled by the move.

"It's alright, just relax, you'll be fine," Ann said reassuringly. Joshua took a deep breath and stared at James. When his thoughts settled, he quietly muttered the words "My son," as tears came to his eyes. But it was only a second before he cleared his throat and shook his head to regain composure.

The visit was pleasant, but the conversation quite guarded. Ann appreciated John's presence. Most of the time he was in the room with them, adding a layer of caution to all that was said. After James' bath, Ann offered the group some tea and cake.

"I see you're back to work at the mill," Joshua said to start some discussion.

"Yes. I took as much time off as I dare, not wanting to give Joe a reason to replace me." James was dozing, giving the adults freedom to discuss other things going on in their lives.

"How's your father doing?" Ann asked, not only due to a genuine desire to know but to set some background to the real question on her mind.

"It appears he only has days left. He hasn't eaten anything for over a week, and he is in and out of consciousness," Joshua weakly replied, being reminded of the mortality of all.

"John, Joshua and I need to talk. Would you please go to the farm and get two pints of milk?" Ann asked, nodding towards the door.

"I'll be there tomorrow. I can get it then. Oh, right. I'll get it now," John said as he realized Ann now wanted a little privacy.

"What do you think about us, Joshua?" Ann said slowly after John had left, purposely keeping the brakes on her real feelings and emotion. She got right to the point, without being cynical. She continued when there was no immediate response from Joshua, "I'm going to be as open and straightforward as I can be. I've accepted the role of raising this child without your help. I'm as much to blame for becoming pregnant as you are. I'm not looking for any revenge or payback in any way. I want you to be part of this family. James needs you as part of this family. But until you are ready to make that commitment, I won't confuse this child with a half-hearted idea of what a father should be. Do you see my point?" Joshua stared at the floor and nodded acknowledgment to Ann's question. She continued, "I'm glad you came today. You needed to meet James and see what a precious little boy he is. I'm glad he is mine. Whether he's ours, is up to you."

Silence. Ann was near bouncing in her chair, but kept control and remained still. She had learned that sometimes to say nothing leaves the most powerful impression. After several minutes of the most severe quiet Joshua had ever experienced, he opened his mouth and squeaked through the first few words, "I'd better start back before it gets too late," as he hands James back to Ann.

"Too late for what?" Ann thought, *"It's barely past noon on a Sunday."*

Joshua walked to the door, opened it, stepped through then turned around staring at the floor and said, "I've enjoyed seeing James and being with you today, Ann. You've given me a lot to think about." He only glanced at her, not able to abide her penetrating stare. Then turned and slowly walked away. As he did so, he was a bundle of conflicting turmoil. In his heart, he felt the gravitational pull of "his family," not his parents' family, but his family. At the same time, he felt inclined to elude the responsibility of being a husband and father. The conflicting

64

emotions rendered his typical macho display into confetti.

To Ann, it was a joy to have Joshua there, playing with James and conversing with her and John. But the ache inside grew as he walked away. She immediately questioned herself, "Was I too hard on him? Did I set too high a goal? No, he needs to make up his mind to be a father, or I'd rather not have him around". But her determination did nothing to ease the pain she felt at his leaving.

CHAPTER

12

"Come in, Jenny," Ann hollered to Jenny knocking at the door while she finished dressing James before leaving for work. "I'd rather stay and play, James. But we both like to eat, and it seems the only way I can buy food is if I leave and go to work." Ann talked to James while dressing him but now turned her attention to Jenny for some last-minute instructions as she wrapped up some cheese, an apple, and some pork John had brought home and cooked the night before. These items would be her simple lunch for the day. "James has had his nappy changed, has been fed and should settle down to sleep for another hour or so. I may be a bit later tonight. Being summer with longer daylight, Joe is putting some pressure to put in extra time. So far, I've resisted, but I sense he'll press for it again today."

"We'll just keep playing until you get home," Jenny replied. This arrangement with Jenny was turning out to be a good fit. With no children of her own, she was enjoying tending James and watching him grow. As Ann exited the front door, John came bounding down the stairs, greeted Jenny and James, and started rustling his breakfast before he left for the farm.

He was working full time now, and his duties had been increased to include most everything done on the farm, including driving a team of horses while hauling grain to town. He also helped butcher the pigs, sheep, and chickens when it was time. John liked farming, but some days while doing something tedious and monotonous like plowing or planting, he would think about changing jobs. The only other jobs John considered were working in the cotton mills or the coal mines. They were always looking for additional labor. Even though he would need training, John would quickly be hired. Both of those jobs paid better than he was earning on the farm. The farmer he worked for realized this and explained he couldn't pay any more right now but offered to give John a positive reference as to his abilities and dependability should he decide to change jobs. Two factors weighed heavily for staying on the farm; variety and working outside. Both other jobs were essentially in non-changing environments, and the task remained the same, day after day, year after year. On the farm, his daily duties changed with the season, and there were babies born; calves, piglets, lambs, and chicks. He liked being out in the weather where he could see the sun and feel the rain. Even when he worked all day in the cold and wet, he felt great satisfaction in sitting by the fire for the evening, warming up.

Ann arrived at the mill a bit early, as she usually did. When the starting bell rang, most of the others were still scurrying to their stations or arranging the mounds of carded cotton fibers near their stations, but Ann's wheel was spinning, producing thread already. Joe began making his starting rounds of the spinning stations as he did each morning immediately after the beginning bell. It was his way of being the taskmaster, like cracking a whip above the heads of a team of oxen. It helped to get everyone up to speed. When he came to Ann, he caught her eye and only said, "See me on your way to lunch. I have something I want to talk to you about." Ann nodded, keeping up her hand-dance with the fibers and spindle. The routine had become so automatic, she even found this same motion occurring in her dreams at night.

"What could he want?" she thought as he walked away. *"He didn't seem angry or upset."* Ann started shuffling through the past several days and weeks to see if she could recall some infraction or oversight. She came up with nothing. Her thought continued, *"In fact, his tone sounded like he had some suggestion or negotiation in mind. What could he want?"*

Ann thought of three possibilities. Joe had recently hired two new spinsters who had been trained at their former mill to spin wool. Making the transition to cotton was proving difficult for them. Perhaps Joe wanted Ann to give them some help. Or maybe Joe wanted Ann to change the location of her wheel. Her current location was near a row of windows, and a couple of the older spinsters' eyesight was deteriorating, so they needed better light to keep spinning. Or perhaps, and she thought this the most likely, Joe wanted Ann to put in more hours. For the next six to eight weeks, there would be enough light to put in another two hours a day. Ann had become one of the top producers on the floor. She knew cotton cloth was in high demand, which meant the need for thread was good as well. The mill owners were pressuring the manager and foreman to find ways to increase production. There was even talk that the owners were considering installing a steam engine to drive the looms in another year.

As the spinsters were leaving the floor for lunch, Ann held back wanting to be the last one leaving so the others wouldn't know Joe had asked her to stay.

"Ann, I'd like you to work an extra two hours each day through the summer. I know you're a little reluctant to stay longer, so I've been authorized to make it more attractive. I'll pay you your regular pay plus and extra shilling an hour for the extra time," Joe said.[4]

The offer of extra pay surprised Ann. She was prepared to resist any offer or demand to put in extra time because of James. She felt she was cheating him being gone from home so much and she felt cheated as well. The last few months had dramatically altered her attitude about what kind of person she was and her feelings now about being a mother. A year ago, she would have never dreamed of having such strong feelings about her family. Her family had become the priority. Before James, she had gone to work to support herself and improve her situation in life. Since James was born, she went to work to improve his life. What she did for work was secondary. It was only a way to acquire the things needed for his health and comfort.

"Joe, I appreciate the offer. I wasn't expecting it. I'll have to think about it until tomorrow," she stammered.

"Sure, I understand. I know that James' babysitter is a factor as well." Joe wanted to let Ann know he was aware that James' well-being and care was a big part of her decision. "It's hot now being summer, but the extra money would be good to buy a better supply of coal to keep your place warmer this winter." Joe wanted to instill the thought that more money would be good for James.

That evening after dinner, James had been put to bed for the night. John was sitting on the porch whittling a new handle for a pitchfork at the farm. Ann came out to join him. They often talked about the latest new thing James was doing or issues concerning the house or work. Tonight, work was the main topic.

"Joe asked me to put in more hours at the mill during the summer," Ann began.

"You've been expecting that. What did you tell him?" John casually asked.

"He's added an incentive. He said he'll pay me an extra shilling an hour for the extra hours I put in," Ann said.

John's eyes grew wide. He quit whittling, "What did you tell him?"

"I told him I'd let him know tomorrow. John, this changes everything. He is asking me to put in extra hours. He's not telling me I have to put in extra hours," Ann explained.

John shrugged his shoulders, "I see the difference you're talking about, but I don't understand why that is so important."

"Let me back up a step to explain. When there are more workers asking for jobs than there are jobs available, the managers can be picky about which workers they'll hire They can tell them how long to work. The workers know if they don't do what they are asked, the managers can easily hire someone else who will. When there is more work than there are workers to do it, the workers have more say in how long they want to work without fear of being replaced because there are not enough good workers available to replace them." John nodded his head to indicate he sort of understood Ann's explanation. She continued, "Since Joe asked me to put in more hours and even offered to pay more for the extra time, it means I can do what I want and not what he wants me to."

John tried to work his way through Ann's reasoning and finally got to the question, "So, does all this mean you're going to put in the extra time or not?"

Ann relaxed, sat back in her chair and let out a big sigh, "Almost every day we talk about something new that James is doing. It's wonderful to see him grow. In the next few months, he'll start crawling and doing other things he's not doing now. I don't want to miss that. I feel bad already about the hours I spend away from him. At the end of the work day, I can't wait to get home and see what is happening." Ann paused, John was wondering if that was her answer. She finally continued, "No, I'm not going to put in the extra hours. I'm one of the best spinsters on the floor. I intend on continuing to be one of the best. They'll have to find another way to get the additional production they want."

Ann was not looking forward to telling Joe her decision. She arrived at the mill 15 minutes before work to give him her answer. "I've done a good job for you, Joe, and I'll keep doing a good job. Work is important, but there is a point when other things -- when other people -- become more important. I need to be home with James as much as possible. I won't be putting in the extra time." Ann stood still and braced herself for a harsh response.

"I don't blame you, Ann," Joe replied. Ann tried not to look surprised at his answer. "I had to ask," he continued. "The manager insisted. I'll ask some of the others for the extra time, but most others' time is not worth the extra pay. It will make my job easier if you don't say anything about it to anyone else."

"What will they do if they can't get the extra production?" Ann asked, treading into territory seldom discussed with the workers.

"In the short-term, they'll lose some orders. They'll fuss about it, but it's a good problem to have -- too many orders. That's better than too few orders. If they think lots of orders will continue, they'll look at expanding or trying some of that new steam-driven machinery," Joe explained.

"From what I've heard, that will cut the number of workers needed," Ann said with some alarm.

"That's what I hear as well, more production with fewer workers, if it works the way they claim it will," Joe said as they walked out on the floor to start the day.

CHAPTER

13

66 I forgot my hat, John. Would you run back into the house and get it for me?" Ann said as the trio, Ann, James, and John, were walking out to the road on a sunny, fall Sunday. They had decided they couldn't spend the day inside. Finally, the weather was bright and warm after a week of cold, wet days. There had even been a light frost on a couple of nights. They knew more cold weather would not be far off, motivating them to go on a picnic down by Beal River. As they turned down Beal Road towards the river, they didn't notice the tall man walking towards them from the other direction.

"Ann, are you leaving for the day?" Ann was startled to hear someone speak to them and to hear her name. The group stopped short and turned to see who was talking.

"Joshua!" Ann and John said in surprised unison. Ann was carrying James. John carried what was to be their lunch. Ann continued after she collected her thoughts, "We were just leaving to walk up to the river and have a picnic," her mind racing on just how she should handle this surprise visit.

"I'm glad I caught you. I wanted to see you all. You're all looking good," Joshua said as he looked them over closely as if it were an inspection. Then he nodded approvingly.

"Why don't you join us?" Ann said, briefly hesitating, not sure it was the right thing to do in this awkward situation.

Joshua smiled big, which made Ann think it was the right thing to do, "I'd love to if you don't mind."

"John, take the basket back to the house and put in some more meat and bread and a couple more apples," Ann said. John scampered back into the house. "Would you like to hold James?" Ann said after a few uncomfortable, silent moments. She slowly handed James to Joshua as James reached back for his mother, wondering who this man was, but he didn't cry. John returned with the extra food, and they all turned toward the river. When they got to the river, they turned off the road and walked upriver about 100 yards to a spot they had picnicked before. Ann and John had discovered it years earlier on one of their exploration days while living with Uncle Jim. There was a grassy mound next to the river, so it was one of the first places to dry off after rain. Several tall cottonwood trees gave cool shade, and the cloud of mosquitoes and flies had been thinned out by the recent frosts.

As soon as they had the picnic all set out and were enjoying the meal, Joshua became very quiet. "Is something wrong, Joshua?" Ann asked as both she and John noticed the dramatic change in his demeanor.

"Pa died last week," he said quietly, staring at the ground. Then after several deep breaths to control his emotions, "I should be relieved. He had been suffering so much the last several months. We knew it was coming and prayed it wouldn't be drawn out too long. No matter how prepared you think you are, when it happens, it's still a shock to realize he will no longer be there.

You looked forward to sharing your latest news and asking for advice about questions you're facing. You realize we're all going to die sometime. If you've got things to do or decisions to make, you'd better do it before your time passes."

"I'm sorry, Joshua. We all are. I'm sure you greatly valued your relationship with him. You can't help but feel a hole in your life where he used to be," Ann said wondering if this was the motivation for Joshua's visit this morning; a dramatic event that triggered a need to be consoled and supported by others who would understand.

"It's a bit strange, but I haven't seen you at work at all," Ann said to change the subject after a few quiet minutes.

"That's because they asked all the loom operators to put in extra hours because of additional orders. I don't leave the mill till several hours later."

"They asked me to put in extra hours as well, but I turned them down. I needed, rather I wanted, to be home with James. It seems like I see him so little as it is," Ann explained. Ann had made a rhubarb and strawberry pie for the occasion from some rhubarb that had been growing in the yard, and John had brought home a hat full of strawberries from the farm. Joshua couldn't give enough praise for the tasty pie after years of living on his and his housemates' cooking. Everyone was completely satisfied having enjoyed the food, the weather, and the conversation. James had dozed off in the shade of the trees with a slight breeze blowing.

"I have something I want to say to you, Ann," Joshua said as they finished their meal.

John shot Ann a look and said, "I've got a fishing pole stashed over behind that tree. I'll see if the fish are biting."

"I'd like you to stay, John. You need to hear this," Joshua said. "I enjoyed that first visit I made to you and James a few months ago. But more than that, it started feelings that I've never had before. I wrestled with those feelings for weeks, wondering what they were. They wouldn't go away. I finally realized what I was feeling was the need to be part of this family, to make this family, my family. I'm sorry, Ann, it took me so long to grow up. Will you be my wife?"

Ann had been planning this for a year. Every conversation, every encounter had been managed to encourage this very moment, even down to the inflection in her voice as they spoke during the occasional visit since James' birth. Was it deceitful or conniving? Not at all. Just as a farmer prepares the soil, adds nutrients, manages the moisture and monitors the weather so when a seed is planted, it can't help but sprout. Ann's hope was for Joshua to propose. She just didn't know when it would happen.

Ann screamed and jumped into Joshua's arms. John picked up James, who woke up and started to fuss at the commotion. "Yes, I will. Of course, I will." John grinned as he turned away from the raft of kissing and hugging that took place.

CHAPTER

14

Many at the mill had learned, as Ann's pregnancy became evident, that Joshua was the father of her baby. News of Joshua's proposal spread like wildfire. By lunchtime, most of the mill workers knew of the proposal, and many of the spinsters gathered around Ann as soon as the lunch bell rang to give congratulations and well-wishes. There was a similar scene on the loom floor as the loom operators converged around Joshua with lots of back slapping and jesting. When the commotion finally died down, Ann and Joshua made their way to the lunch shed and sat in the very spots they had been more than a year earlier.

"You've made me a happy woman, Joshua," Ann beamed as they grabbed each other's hands.

"I feel like I can finally breathe again," Joshua replied as they unwrapped their lunch and began, or continued, what would become a long-standing tradition; eating lunch while they discussed their future. And right now, there were lots of plans to be made. "It's has taken me too long to realize this is what I want," he continued. Within a few days, they had set a date for their wedding, November 9th, 1797, a Saturday, a little over a month away. Saturday would be a half day of work and the daylight hours would be short enough to curtail the extra time Joshua had been putting in.

After the wedding, Joshua would move into Ann's house. John would be welcome to stay, being his house as well. They even discussed the possibility of Ann eventually quitting work, leaving her free to care for James and keep house. With Joshua and John working, there should be enough income to support the family.

CHAPTER

15

November 9th, the big day finally arrived. Ann had been up most of the night before making sure everyone had clean clothes. After work, there would only be time to come home, get washed up, changed, and get to the church, St Mary's of Oldham. Currently, Oldham was about 12,000 people, including many small surrounding communities. St Mary's Church was built in the 1500s and had already seen two renovation and expansions. There were from two to six weddings per week. Today, Ann and Joshua's wedding was the only one scheduled.

"John is planning on being there, isn't he?" Joshua asked Ann as they hurriedly walked home from the mill, hand in hand.

"Yes, he will be one of the witnesses. We must bring one witness. The Church will supply the other," she replied.

"Witnesses, I hadn't thought about needing a witness. Will Jenny be there?" he asked nervously, having not encountered Jenny since her scathing attack on him at the mill.

"Of course, she'll be there. She wouldn't miss it. She takes credit for you finally marrying me," Ann chuckled while jabbing him in the ribs.

"I won't give her all the credit, but she did help to get me off dead center. Is John aware of the time he needs to be there?" Joshua was finally getting up to speed on the details of the day.

"It was the last thing I said to him this morning before we left the house," Ann said as they approached her home. She could tell Joshua was nervous about facing Jenny, lagging as they walked up to the door of the house. Ann walked in and greeted James and Jenny. She quickly noticed their clothes were sitting out ready to be changed into. Some food for James was packed ready to go. Jenny had Sunday clothes on for the event. "You can change in our room, Joshua," Ann said as she turned around to face Joshua. But Joshua wasn't there. "Joshua, where are you?" she said as Joshua peeked through the door into the house.

"I'm right here. Uh, hi Jenny," he tried not to sound nervous at this first encounter with Jenny since her merciless, verbal assault. But his quivering voice betrayed him as he stood frozen, waiting for Jenny's reaction.

Jenny stood still eyeing him over with no expression on her face. Ann, seeing what appeared to be a stand-off, became alarmed at the prospects of her wedding day turning into a battle scene. For ten long seconds, the chill in the room seemed to crack and crunch like walking on frosty snow in winter. Then Jenny broke out in a big, toothy smile as she shook her head and said, "That was fun!" as she put out her arms, walked to Joshua and gave him a grand hug. "I'm so glad you've finally come to your senses. Welcome to the family."

Joshua stood like a statue with no reaction, not knowing how to interpret what was happening. Then, as he could feel that

Jenny's hug was genuine and comments were sincere, he slowly put one arm around Jenny, venturing cautiously into this new territory.

Ann finally started breathing again. "Now that you two are getting along, where's John? He's not home yet?"

"I haven't seen him," Jenny replied. "I have his clothes all ready for him. He should be here any second."

Ann and Joshua finished changing and getting ready. Everyone was ready to leave for the church, but John still had not arrived. Ann reviewed again in her mind and repeated aloud the exact last words she said to John that morning. As usual, he was sleepy and still waking up, but he repeated the instructions back close enough that she was satisfied he understood the importance of the day's events and schedule.

"We can't wait any longer," Ann explained as she gathered up things and people. "We have a lot to carry with James and his basket of food. We'd better start to the church. John can run over quickly when he gets home. He quite often shows up late saying, 'I had to finish the field' or 'I had some trouble at the end' or some other reason he's late."

It was a 30-minute walk to the church. A group of people, especially with a baby, is always slower than a single individual running or trotting along, able to weave and dodge people and animals on the road. The early November day was cool, cloudy and quite breezy, portending the winter storms that would be arriving in a few weeks. Upon arriving at the church, the group entered to find it empty as expected with no other weddings scheduled today. Jenny and James settled into a pew near the back to rest from their walk while Ann and Joshua went to find the priest and review the arrangements for the day. They found him in his office.

"Come in. You seem out of breath. Sit down so we can review some details. Is everyone here?" he asked.

"All except John, my brother. He is going to be one of the witnesses. Is the church supplying the other witness?" Ann inquired.

"Yes, Ralph will be the other witness. He is the groundskeeper and serves as the Recorder here at the Church. He also is usually one of the witnesses since he is here all the time. He keeps a clean set of clothes to change into for weddings," the priest explained seeing that Ann became concerned that a groundskeeper, a potentially dirty groundskeeper, would be a witness at her wedding. "I asked Ralph to get cleaned up about an hour ago. I'm sure he's ready. We'll wait a few more minutes for John to come. We'll start as soon as he arrives."

Ann and Joshua joined the group waiting in the chapel and reported all was ready, except for John. Two arguments were bouncing back and forth in Ann's mind, *"Why couldn't he be on time, today of all days,"* followed by, *"I'm sure he has a good reason for being late."* After a few minutes, the priest and Ralph came into the chapel ready to proceed.

"John is not here yet?" asked the Priest. Ann shrugged her shoulders and shook her head. "We can't wait any longer. Both Ralph and I have other appointments shortly. Do you have someone else who could be a witness?"

"We have Jenny. Could Jenny be the other witness?" Ann asked.

"I'm afraid not," replied the Priest, "A witness has to be a man," he said apologetically, eyeing Jenny holding James.

His answer pushed Ann over the edge as the stress and frustrations of the day overcame her. "What? A woman can't be a witness? God has determined women have the babies, enduring more pain than most men will have in a lifetime. I'm to nurture, teach and raise that child to be a man, so the man can dictate a woman can't be a simple witness at a wedding?" The stress and anxiety she had tamped down and contained now came raging out, dripping from her tongue on the hapless priest. "Does it say in the Bible that only men can be witnesses? Mathew chapter18 does say we need to have two witnesses, but nowhere that I know of does it say they must be men. Women can work to put food on the table to feed your belly. Women earn money to pay debts. You'll take the money women put in the plate that's passed around every Sunday. But you won't let a woman be a witness at a wedding? Something does not make sense here," Ann took a breath and gathered her thoughts as the priest could only nod and wither.

Just then the front door banged open and the overweight, out of shape wife of the farmer where John worked came in. "There's been an accident. John is hurt, but I think he'll be alright," she said gasping, getting only two or three words out per breath. "Let me sit down to catch my breath, and I'll say more." She collapsed onto the nearest pew, put her head down and continued breathing heavily. The group immediately gathered around her, anxious to hear about the accident but was restrained enough to allow her a brief rest before pressing for more details.

She continued, "John was hurrying to unhook the horses from the wagon and put them in the pasture before leaving to come to the wedding. As he was gathering up the harnesses, he walked around behind our big mare and bent down to pick up something he'd dropped on the ground. That spooked the horse, and she kicked John, catching him across his forehead. He flipped a complete somersault, landing on his back, out cold and bleeding badly. I was sent to get the doctor while my husband tried to stop the bleeding and wake him up. Head wounds are especially bloody you know," she added. Now that she had caught her breath, she felt to add a little commentary to the event. "By the time I got back with the doc, John was awake. The doc stitched him up. It was about a two-inch gash. By then, John wanted to try to stand up. He could stand up alright, but he couldn't walk without falling over. My husband said he'd lead him home on the horse, and I'd better scurry over here cause you'd be wondering."

Everyone felt relief that John appeared he would recover. The doctor had examined him, and the farmer was accompanying him home to rest.

"Perhaps we should go and check on him," suggested Jenny.

All eyes looked to Ann for a response to Jenny's suggestion. Ann knew it was her decision to make. It was her wedding day. She looked around the room. Joshua was there. Jenny and James were there. They were at the church. The priest and Ralph were there. There had been a mountain of effort to get everyone and everything to this point. In a few minutes the wedding ceremony could be accomplished. If the wedding was delayed, she feared there would always be another reason to keep them from being married. But the dilemma of a witness still was not solved.

"James is a man," Ann shouted.

"Yes, but he's just a baby," the priest countered.

"You said a witness had to be a man. James is a man. A witness observes an event. James will surely observe this event. He may not understand it, but I don't understand your prayers in Latin either, but you want me to believe they're effective in my behalf," Ann debated.

"But how will he sign the wedding register?" the Priest contended.

"The same way that Joshua and I will sign, with an X, with a witness noting whose X it is."

The priest could only roll his eyes and nod in agreement. After a short ceremony, Ralph asked the bride, groom, and witness over to his desk to sign the wedding register. Ann and Joshua both made their X. Then Ann put the pen in James tiny hand, folded her hand around his hand and the pen, and made a similar X as a witness to the wedding. Ralph then added his notation as to whose X it was.

"That's the first time I've seen that happen, a child, an infant being witness to the wedding of his parents," Ralph said.

As the wedding party walked towards home, with Joshua carrying James, reveling in the thought they were now a family. "This will certainly be a day to remember," Joshua remarked.

"I feel like we've finally reached the top of the mountain after fighting through a rocky, twisted trail," Ann replied.

When they got home, they found John sitting at the table, picking at the roast chicken that was to be the wedding dinner. "We heard what happened," Ann said sitting at the table next to John. "How do you feel now?'

"I'm still a bit dizzy, but I'm better than when I got home. I'll probably be much better in the morning. But my head sure hurts," John said slowly.

"Did the doc give you anything for the pain," asked Ann.

"Oh, yeah, it's in my pocket," he said as he fished out a dark brown bottle and handed it to Ann. Ann smiled and nodded as she read the label on the bottle, "LAUDANUM".

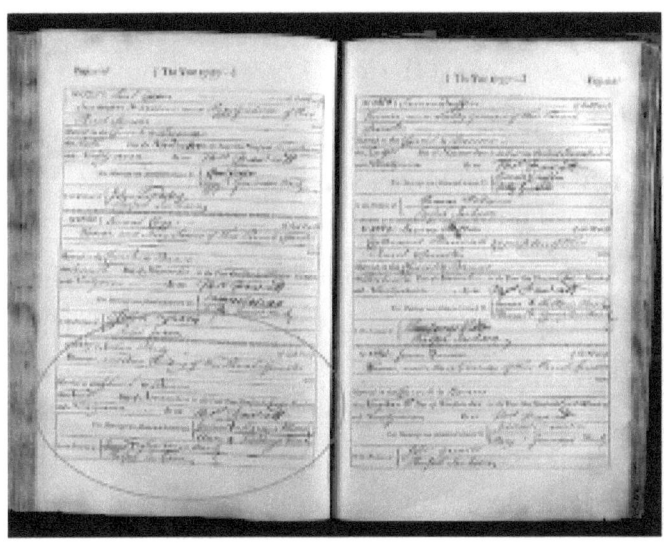

Hardy-Fielding Marriage Record
Reproduced by kind persmission of *Ancestry.com* who own the
copyright to this image.

Manchester, England, Church of England Marriages and Banns, 1754-1930 for Ann Fielding

Record Index

    Name: Ann Fielding
    Birth Year:
    Age:
    Marriage Date: 6 Nov 1797
    Parish: Oldham, St Mary
  Parish as It Appears: Oldham
    Father:
  Spouse Father:
Reference Number: QB/127.L185/1/53
    Item Number:
    Archive Roll:

Source Information

Record URL: http://search.ancestry.com/cgi-bin/sse.dll?
indiv=1&dbid=ManchesterMarriagesORCMI=72073&

Source Information: Ancestry.com. Manchester,
England, Church of England Marriages and Banns, 1754-
1930 [database online]. Provo, UT, USA: Ancestry.com
Operations, Inc., 2013.
Original data: Anglican Parish Registers. Manchester,
England: Manchester Libraries, Information and Archives.
Image produced by permission of Manchester City
Council. Images may be used only for the purposes of the
family history research in accordance with Ancestry's
website terms of use. At the request of the Manchester
Diocese it is highlighted that the use of images for
retrospective or proxy baptism is not permitted.

Hardy-Fielding Marriage Record Locator
Reproduced by kind persmission of *Ancestry.com* who own the
copyright to this image.

(The Year 1797-)

No 1327} Joshua Hardy ------------------------- of this Parish
Weaver, and Ann Fielding of this Parish Spinster

-- were
Married in this Church by Banns ------------------------------
This Ninth Day of November in the Year One Thousand Seven
Hundred
And Ninety-seven -----By me   Mos Fawcett

This Marriage was Solemnized   { Joshua X Hardy's Mark
                  between Us   { Ann X Fielding's Mark
           In the Presence of { James X Fielding's Mark
                               { Ralph Jackson

CHAPTER

16

A little over a month later, the family was having a birthday dinner to celebrate James' one-year birthday. Jenny was there as well.

"Jenny, Joshua and I have been talking about me quitting work and staying home. With both he and John making wages, we think I won't need to work," Ann said as they put the finishing touches on the meal for the day.

"I knew this day would come soon," Jenny responded. "I've enjoyed watching James grow and learn to do new things. I'll miss him. I'll miss you all."

The next day at the mill, Ann arrived a few minutes earlier than her usual time. "Joe, I'm going to quit at the end of the week," Ann said, about a month after the wedding.

Joe got a pained look on his face, then said with a pleading look in his eyes, "Please Ann, could you hang on for a couple more months? I've been expecting you'd quit one of these days, but I'd like to keep you working as long as I can." Ann said nothing and shook her head, refusing his offer. "OK, what if I raised your pay a shilling a day? Would you stay a bit longer then?"

It didn't take long for Ann to realize this would bring her

pay to nearly a Pound a week, no small consideration. In the next moment, she considered James, weighing the pros and cons of extra time with him, versus the extra pay. She paused briefly, but still concluded to spend the time with James. "I'm sorry Joe, that is a good offer, a serious offer, but James is only a baby once. This week will be my last week."

"I don't blame you," said Jim, yielding to the fact that he would be losing one of his best workers. "I had to ask. I figured when you and Joshua got married it wouldn't be long before we'd have this conversation. You're not the teenager you were when you started here. A husband and a child change your view of life and your priorities. I've been a bachelor, then married, now single again."

Ann was surprised, "I didn't know you were married. I don't think anyone on the floor knows."

"There is one who knows, Mary at station 3. She was my wife."

Now Ann was surprised, "Mary, isn't she the one you hired not too long ago that used to spin wool? One of those who would rather be close to the window for better light?

Joe chuckled with a slight grin, "That's right. It's better if no one knows. Will you keep it that way?"

Ann nodded. "It's a shame it didn't work out."

"It's my fault. I've been regretting it ever since," Joe explained. "I got too comfortable with the way life was going and had an affair with another spinster to add some excitement. Then I started lying to cover it up. Once we couldn't trust each other, the marriage fell apart in a hurry." Ann was surprised he was sharing such personal information with her. Joe was too. But with Ann leaving shortly, he didn't think it mattered much now.

The transition to married life was rather rocky for both Ann and Joshua. It wasn't surprising, considering they both had been on their own for decades. Other than their bosses at work, they each had been deciding what their priorities and schedules were. Plus, they decided what they did on their time off. Ann had made many adjustments in caring for James and his needs on his schedule. Bigger changes were necessary when Joshua joined the family. There were schedule considerations, food preferences.

After a few weeks of a verbal tug-of-war, the tension finally boiled over. Without telling Ann of his intentions, Joshua went to the pub with some of his friends from the mill one Saturday and arrived home in the early morning. His condition was not the best. As he staggered into bed, Ann wanted to address the matter right then but could see the effort was futile until Joshua had a clearer head.

The next morning was Sunday. Joshua slept late. He finally got up at nearly noon and went looking for some breakfast. Ann said little, fixed him some breakfast and waited until he had finished. Knowing he was hung over from the drinking, she sat down at the table and spoke in a soft but firm voice. "Joshua, this will not do," she said. Even speaking in a soft voice caused him pain. Talking about his behavior now would make a lasting impression on him, she reasoned. "When James was born, my priorities changed dramatically. My nights out with the girls, drinking and dancing, stopped. Why? Because I now had more important things to do that mattered and would continue to matter for the rest of my life. I don't mind you going out with the boys occasionally, but we need to know where you'll be and when you'll be home. You are our provider. You keep us safe. We love you. Let's keep it that way."

Ann got up and started cleaning up Joshua's dishes. There was no shouting nor arguing. The pain in Joshua's head was now eclipsed by the pain in his heart as he realized his error. The way his life had been for over thirty years was not the way it was now. He must move ahead and let go of the past. Ann made it clear he did not have to cut off his friends, but he needed to make ample room for those in his life that were now more important.

CHAPTER

17

With James and now Joshua added to the household, John was feeling crowded. Nothing was said, and every effort was made to accommodate him in the family. As James got older, he gravitated to sleeping in John's room. At times, John was bothered that he needed to accommodate these extra people in his house. After all, wasn't it he and Ann who located the old abandon family home? Didn't he help fix it up over several years? He felt it was his home. But he couldn't fault Ann for the family she now had. One day the farmer where John worked suggested he sleep in the storage shed during lambing season. The expectant ewes need to be checked on several times through the night. John jumped on the proposal and even suggested, that with a little fixing, he could make the shed into a home. He would stay there as long as he worked for the farmer.

The farmer quickly saw the advantage of having John living at the farm year around. As the farmer got older and could accomplish less and less in a day, John was eager to assume a bigger role in running of the farm.

"I have some news I need to share," John said as they finished supper one night. "I've decided to move out."

"What brought this on?" asked Ann.

"It started when I was asked to stay and sleep at the farm in a storage shed during lambing season so I'd be available through the night should a ewe need my help. After looking over the shed carefully, I realized it wouldn't take much to make it a livable home if it was just me."

"Is it because James sleeps most of the time in your room now?" questioned Ann.

"I do my best not to snore," added James who was nearing twelve and growing near an inch a month now.

"It's none of that," responded John. "Your family is growing. If I move out, James and I both get a separate room. Plus, I can check on the ewes and other stock as needed through the night without disturbing somebody else."

Two weeks later, John brought home the farmers wagon used to haul grain and butchered meat to town. The family spent the evening loading up Johns belongings.

"I'm only moving a couple miles away," John said to a sullen Ann as they loaded up the last of his things. "I hope I'm still welcome at Sunday dinner."

"I'll be angry if you don't come," responded Ann as she wiped away a tear.

Why are you crying? I'm going less than 2 miles away," John asked.

"Don't you see what this means?" Ann weakly said. "We're getting older. Life is changing. Life has changed. I raised you and you're leaving. I'm the only mother you've ever known. You're leaving our home.

John nodded but remained silent. What Ann was saying was true. Uncle Jim had shown them great kindness, but he would always be the uncle with his own family. Ann and John were a separate family. And now Ann and Joshua has their family.

"We've grown up together," John finally said. "Remember when we first discovered this house while living with Uncle Jim? Then we decided to clean it up and fix it up with discarded furniture we found in garbage piles? We were only 10 or 12."

"A couple of years after we found this house, I started work at the mill and decided we were grown up enough to move out of Uncle Jim's and be on our own," Ann continued to reminisce. "We had a few rough times. It wasn't easy becoming a woman with no mother around. And you were becoming a man. We discovered things that we'd only heard rumors about. We made plenty of mistakes. We also had plenty of good times, happy times." Ann became too emotional to say more. They looked at each other lost in the thoughts of two decades of memories. Then, as if on cue, each broke out in a big smile, then chuckles as they both became aware they had reached a milestone in their lives. They had passed the test and achieved victory over adolescences.

"Even though we never knew Ma and Pa, I can feel their pride looking down on us," Ann finally said.

"I was thinking the same thing," added John. "I feel they're pleased with what we've done with our lives so far."

They cautiously wrapped their arms around each other,

cautious because they had never had hugged or shown that type of emotion. They were too busy avoiding the thorns and sharp rocks of life. Too busy planning ahead. Do we have enough food? Will the roof make it through the winter? Do we have enough wood or coal to get through the winter? A sweet feeling swept over them as they paused, took a breath and reveled in the unique bond between a brother and sister.

CHAPTER

18

James was considered the champ at mumblety-peg, at least on his street. At nearly twelve years of age, mumblety-peg was the perfect game as boys were shedding the remaining ties of the apron strings and exploring that vast, rough, and unpredictable landscape known as adolescence. How could it not be the perfect game? It included an ample supply of two essential ingredients, knives and challenging other boys.

Many variations of the game have been played, but the basic version that James was acquainted with was as follows; two boys stand face to face about an arm's length apart. Their feet spread to shoulder distance. The first player throws the knife, trying to stick the blade into the ground a few inches to a foot or more from the other boy's foot. If the blade sticks, the other boy must move his foot to where the knife stuck in the ground. If the blade does not stick, no movement is required. The farther you throw the knife, the harder it is to make it stick. Then the other boy has a turn. The object of the game is to keep increasing the stance of the other boy until he can no longer reach the required stretch or he falls over. The key is to be consistently able to throw the knife variable distances and have it stick blade first in the ground while balancing precariously with feet spread wide apart.

When the weather was good and the chores were done, boys

would gather near the river to challenge each other. The winner would continue playing challenger after challenger until he was beaten. That established a new champion. The champion who had just lost could immediately re-challenge to see if the new champion was good enough to retain his title.

"I challenge you to a game," called Bob as soon as he rounded the corner and James was within earshot. Two other boys were with Bob, who had also given James healthy competition the day before. In fact, he wouldn't admit it, but James had been a little worried at one point he may lose his title.

"I've been waiting for you to show up," countered James. "I was beginning to think I beat you so badly yesterday, you went home to lick your wounds and wouldn't show up today." Being able to stick a knife in the ground accurately was only half the game. The other half was who could out-insult the other guy. It was all part of the game and made for a stirring encounter.

James hadn't noticed when the group was approaching, but tagging along about 30 feet behind was another person, a girl younger than the other boys. She didn't say anything nor did any of the boys mention her or who she was, but was interested in the activity and observed quietly.

"After your poor showing yesterday, I'll give you first throw," said James and the game was on as he taunted his opponent. Bob's first throw was good, and James had to lengthen his stretch about 18 inches, which worried him. Today Bob might prove to be the one to take his title. James decided to "swallow the whale," a phrase used to indicate he was betting the whole game on his one throw, sometimes referred to as "betting the farm."

To do this, James would have to sink his knife far enough from Bob's foot that there would be no way he could reach it, thus losing the game. James held the knife by the point and aimed it five feet to the right of Bob. Then, just to antagonize him, he focused at a point five feet to the left, all the time emitting mumbling sounds and screwing up his face as if he was doing some serious calculations. It was all part of the game and was meant to intimidate the challenger. He aimed to the right again, this time closing one eye as if he was aiming a gun.

"Just throw the blasted knife!" shouted Bob after enduring several minutes of the charade.

"I'm just assessing how bad to beat you," replied James. The longer he took the bigger the triumph, or defeat if he missed the throw. It was all part of why James was so popular in the neighborhood. He took the knife by the point, quickly looked to Bob's left and in classic style, let it fly. The blade shot through the air did a complete 180-degree spin and sank deep into the ground. The rest of the group who had arrived with Bob, and up to this point was rooting for him, let out a whoop and cheer at both the style of the throw and the risk James took in throwing it.

"I want to challenge James," shouted one boy.

"After me," insisted the other boy as he pulled the knife out of the ground and took his position in front of James. James had held the title for so long it was becoming somewhat of a status symbol to play him and to get beat by him.

In playing the next two boys, James employed a different tactic. Instead of throwing long shots to eliminate them quickly, he threw many short shots, drawing the challengers into a deeper and deeper stretch until they were almost doing the splits. They became unstable and between the pain of being stretched out so far and struggling to maintain their balance, they fell over. James remained cool through the competition. Looking around after the second boy lost he said, reveling in his victory, "Are there any other takers?"

From the perimeter of the group came a small, high-pitched voice, "I'll challenge you." The group broke into sneers and chuckles when they realized it was coming from the girl who had tagged along behind Bob and his friends.

"Go on home and leave us alone," Bob asserted. "I said you could come only if you didn't bother us."

"You know her?" asked James.

"Yah, she's my cousin who's visiting here with her mum," Bob answered, then directed his comments to the girl, "We've got serious business going on here and can't be distracted by a nine-year-old girl," as if a three-year difference in age was too vast to tolerate. Bob was clearly annoyed at several things; that he had to bring her along in the first place and now she was taking James' attention. Probably most of all, that he had lost his challenge to James and now she wanted a shot at beating him. "What makes you think James would even waste his time with a challenge from you?"

"What's your name?" James asked the girl.

"Ann, Ann Henthorn," she replied.

"Ann. Same as my mother. What makes you think you can

beat me? Have you ever thrown a knife?" James asked as the other boys paced around disgusted at not being the focus of the conversation.

"It looks simple enough. I could probably do it," she said as the boys rolled their eyes and shook their heads in disbelief.

"OK. Give it a try," James said, handing her the knife.

"What are you doing?" Bob shouted incredulously. "She's just a kid. She probably injures herself with her fork when she eats her beans, and you're handing her your knife?"

James was enjoying the reaction from the other boys. Ann took the knife by the handle and made an awkward swinging motion with her arm, at the end of which the knife dropped out of her hand landing flat on the ground. The boys let out a hoot and several other disgusting noises.

"I've had enough," announced Bob. "Come on Ann. We're going home," as he and the boys made strides for home.

Ann took a few steps, hesitated, turned and said, "Thanks, James. Sorry I didn't do better," then trotted off to catch up with the others.

James watched her leave and thought, *"She's just a kid, but I like her. She's got spunk."*

CHAPTER
19

Joshua and James sat at the table, trying desperately to wake up. Joshua needed to be to work at the mill shortly. James wanted to start weeding the garden before it got hot. Ann had been up long enough to make some coffee and was frying four eggs for her men, who were particular about their eggs; yokes not runny, but not hard either. The instructions were they had to "glisten". She stood there, utensil in hand, poised over the pan, ready to scoop the eggs out on a plate the second they reached the perfect degree of doneness.

As she stood there, hand hovering in the air over the pan, James noticed something for the first time. Ann appeared to be a little plumper. It shocked him. His mother had changed only slightly, but he had a fixed image in his mind of his mother. He never realized that image might change. Why should it surprise him? He had change a lot during the last five years. He was nearly fourteen and certainly had noticed changes in his body the last few months. He was growing. He had become more muscular. Oh, and hair! Why was hair appearing at strange places, armpits, on his face, even a few strands on his chest and other areas? Joshua had teased him a time or two about hair appearing on his upper lip.

The first awareness of his mother changing evolved into the question as to why? Life was good. Joshua's income seemed to be sufficient for them to live comfortably. James noticed most people gained weight as they got older. *"How old would she be?"* he asked himself. James was getting better with numbers, and he was making an effort to learn. *"I understand mum was 18 years old when I was born,"* he thought to himself. *"I'm fourteen years old now. That would make mum...,"* as the calculations continued in his mind, he finished his breakfast. He scooped up the last bite of eggs and some bread and arrived at his answer. *"She's over thirty! Wow, she's getting old."*

"I noticed this morning, it looks like mum has put on some weight," James casually said to Joshua as they went out the door together. After he said it, he realized it might not have been a good thing to ask. Joshua may scold him.

Instead, Joshua looked at him with a big grin and said, "Mention it later today to your mum. There is a reason for it. I think she'll have something to tell you."

Joshua left for the mill, and James went out in the yard where they had built a little farm yard with a collection of animals. They had rabbits and a dozen chickens. The chickens supplied the eggs for breakfast each morning. They weren't penned or fenced in; rather they were kept close simply by scattering a small cup of barley on the ground each morning and evening. The barley wasn't sufficient to satisfy them but was enough to get them scratching and looking for additional seeds, bugs, and worms. The rabbits and chickens provided most of the meat portion of their diet. On special occasions, Ann would buy a piece of pork or beef and roast it. They also had a garden and raised some potatoes, carrots, peas, corn, strawberries, and rhubarb. It was James' job to keep the weeds hoed. The planting and harvesting were a family affair.

"Mum," James started as he realized he might be treading on thin ice. But Joshua's helpful response that morning gave him the courage to continue. "I noticed this morning you've put on some weight. Pa said I should ask you about it."

James braced for a possible reprimand but relaxed when Ann's response was similar to Joshua's. "So you've noticed I've put on weight recently. Well, I'll be putting on a lot more in the next few months."

James was puzzled, "What do you mean? How do you know you'll put on more weight?"

"I'm expecting another baby," Ann said. The announcement was completely unexpected. He assumed their family would always be just the three of them. His initial reaction was to resent this intrusion into their family by another person. They each had their place in the household. Joshua went to work at the mill to make money to buy food and other things. Ann cooked and cleaned the house, mended and sewed the clothes. James tended the animals and the garden. Now somebody else was going to intrude on their little kingdom and throw everything out of balance.

"How do you feel about that?" Ann asked as James stood in stunned silence, trying hard not to show any reaction.

"Will it be a boy or a girl?" questioned James.

"We won't know until it's born," replied Ann softly, seeing

109

James was having some difficulty processing this new information.

"And when will that be?" James continued to explore.

"In about five months," replied Ann.

"Ok." Then veering sharply to another subject, "I'm meeting Bob down by the river." James' response was curt as he quickly left the house and headed towards the river. The truth was, he had no arrangement to meet Bob by the river but rationalized the fib by thinking, *"I'll meet Bob by the river if he happens to walk by."* James needed some time alone to mull over this latest development. The river was always a good place to do that.

The sun had drifted low in the sky when James decided it was about time to head back home. Besides, he was getting hungry. His feelings about the addition to the family had improved. He tried to look on the positive side. *"It would be exciting to have a new little brother or sister in the house. I have a lot I could teach him or her. It would be easier if I knew which it would be, a boy or girl, which would change the lesson plan entirely. Girls usually didn't care about mumblety-peg or fishing and are squeamish around frogs. If it is a girl, I'd have to limit myself to girly stuff, such as cooking and sewing. All things considered, it had better not be a girl,"* he concluded.

CHAPTER
20

Over the next five months, James carefully watch the changes that were happening to his mother. An addition to the family was a new experience for him. As Ann grew larger and more uncomfortable, James tried to take on more of the household chores, such as the mending and some of the cooking. He found he wasn't very good at either, but Ann appreciated his efforts.

"I wish the baby would come so you would feel better," James said to his mum as the family was finishing dinner one night.

"It won't be long now," Ann responded. "Maybe we should talk about when the baby does come." James was not sure what that meant and wasn't certain he wanted to know. Ann continued, "Joshua has arranged for a midwife to come and help deliver the baby when it is born. In fact, it's the same midwife that came when you were born."

"What's a midwife?" James asked.

"It's a woman who delivers babies for a living and knows what to watch for, what to do and what not to do. This midwife is slowing down some and is only helping former customers." James nodded as he was trying to understand this new information.

Ann continued, "Giving birth to a baby can be…," Ann searched for the right words, "it can cause quite a commotion. It would be best if you went to Bob's or maybe Uncle Jim's while the baby is being born. We'll tell you all about it and answer all your questions when you come back."

James realized that was all the information he was going to get at this point. He wasn't sure he wanted any more information. It all sounded mysterious. But his mother said she'd answer all his questions after the baby was born. That was good enough for now.

That night, James lay in his bed reviewing the conversation. He wondered what she meant by "a commotion." Why would she recommend he go to Bob's or Uncle Jim's while the baby was being born? Many nights over the next few weeks, he lay in his upstairs bedroom, windows propped wide open, praying for a breeze from the right direction to cool the room down to sleeping temperature, he replayed his mother's comments over and over.

It all became crystal clear on the 23rd of December. It was a Sunday, a day when Joshua didn't have to rise early to go to work, so the family would lay in bed and extra hour or longer. Sometimes they would go to church, but not lately since Ann was not in any condition to make the walk.

James had risen briefly at his usual time, found a slice of bread to stave off his morning hunger and settled back under the covers. Winter was coming on, so he added an extra blanket to his bed and it sure felt good. He was in a state of mental twilight, not asleep but not awake enough to have anything on his mind.

He was startled to alertness by a shriek from the bedroom downstairs. He thought it sounded vaguely like his mother but couldn't be sure. His mother never raised her voice, except when calling the men to dinner. He listened carefully for clues as to what was happening.

"James, come quickly," Joshua hollered up the stairs. James scrambled and started downstairs but was interrupted by Joshua standing at the bottom. "Get dressed and get the midwife. It's time."

James was starting to understand what his mother meant when she used the word "commotion" in describing the childbirth. Joshua and Ann had explained several months ago, who the midwife was and where she lived. They had even made a point to walk by her house once while on an evening walk to be sure there would be no confusion when the time came. James ran the whole distance there, arriving in less than five minutes. The trip back wasn't nearly as fast as the midwife limped along as best she could. James wanted to help her move faster but didn't know how to accomplish that.

When they arrived back home, the midwife instantly took control of the house, calmly but efficiently directing Joshua to gather several items, assessing Ann's condition and preparing her, the bed, and surroundings for the arrival of a new member of the family.

"Did you bring it?" Ann shouted at the midwife as the next contraction subsided enough to allow her to speak.

"I've got it right here," she responded as she pulled a dark brown bottle from her pocket. "Do you want some now?"

"No, not yet, but keep it close," Ann said through clenched teeth. She then looked at Joshua and nodded towards James.

Joshua understood what she meant and walked over to James, who was standing near the door. "You should spend the day with Bob," He said to James. James looked at his mother, not wanting to leave while she was obviously distressed. "Giving birth is very painful, and it could take several hours. The midwife and I will do all we can to help, but there is only so much we can do," Joshua reasoned. James looked at his mother, who looked back and nodded towards the door, indicating he'd better leave.

As James left the house, the pain, the "commotion" that was evident sparked a new, deeper appreciation for his mother.

James and Bob spent the day down at Beal River exploring and talking. Occasionally some other guys would come by and challenged James. James refused. He knew he'd be off his game today and didn't want to take a chance on a loss today.

"Are you hoping for a brother or a sister?" Bob asked later in the day.

James shrugged and answered, "A brother, of course. I know a lot of stuff that I can teach a brother. But if it's a girl," James paused while he mentally wrestled with the thought of having a sister. "Well, girls are just different."

When the shadows from the tall trees cast shade across the clearing to the other side of the river, James began to shiver. "I guess I better be getting back and see what happened today," he said.

As James walked back, he dreaded what he might find,

recalling the desperate state when he left. He sensed his world would be dramatically different from now on. He shuddered as he pushed open the door and stepped inside. His worries began to melt as his mother, hearing him come in, softly called out, "James, come see the new baby."

James walked to where he could see the bundle his mother was holding. The midwife was gone, and Joshua was seated next to the bed looking quite pleased and relaxed. Ann folded back several layers of blanket allowing James a good look. He had never seen a newborn or an infant before. Whatever he was expecting, this was not it. He was startled and tried to control his reaction, but caught himself, mouth open, and only part words and stutters escaping through his seized throat. The baby's head was still misshapen from the birth, eyelids puffed up like balls of cotton and only occasional strands of colorless hair strewn across a bald head.

Ann, seeing his shock, was quick to add, "She'll look better tomorrow. Her name is Sarah."

It was too much for James to take in. He tried to smile, then backed out of the room, out the front door and sat on the step. Breathing deeply to calm himself, attempting to settle the picture of the baby in his mother's arms. He must now share his mother with another person, and that other person is a girl!

The next day, James was unsure how to act around his expanded family. Finally, his mother called him to her. "James, Sarah has just been changed and fed. Would you like to hold her and rock her to sleep?"

"If you think I can," James replied hesitantly. He carefully, slowly took her in his arms and sat in the chair next to the bed. A wave of relief washed over him as he looked at her and realized she looked very different from the day before. After a few minutes watching her drift off to sleep, he quietly said, "She's beautiful, Mum."

CHAPTER

21

In the early 1800s, young men would often enter the workforce about age 14, if not earlier. Young women would start work under unusual circumstances, as in Ann's case, having no parents. Most people scoffed at education. Most jobs didn't require one to read or write, and only the most basic of math was needed to understand the cost of items or rate of pay. Most adults could neither read nor write their whole life. It was no different in the Joshua Hardy home as evidenced by the "X" representing their signatures on the wedding record. The type of work James might pursue had been the occasional subject at the dinner table for a couple of years. It was exciting for James to anticipate entering the workforce leaving, for the most part, boyhood games.

"Go to work with me at the mill tomorrow," Joshua said to James one night as they were finishing dinner. "If you stay out of the way, the floor boss won't mind. I know of no better way to learn about the work than being right there where it's happening. Of course, you couldn't start as a loom operator, but spending the day there would give you a good idea what the work is like."

By this time, the mill had converted to steam-driven looms. Instead of weaving one three-foot wide bolt of cloth, a loom operator could run several looms at a time. Steam power did the heavy, tedious work. Joshua carefully watched his looms operate, looking for snags or broken threads or anything that would ruin the cloth. He also made constant fine adjustments to maximize the efficiency of the loom. There was also the needed heddle adjustments to change the patterns in the material.

The next morning, Ann was engulfed in a mixture of pride and sadness as Joshua and James left the house, even though it was just for the day for James. To Ann, it was the end of James' boyhood. All Ann could see were two silhouettes as they entered the roadway in the early morning dawn. James was just as tall as Joshua but much skinnier. He may still grow an inch or two in the years to come. Joshua had gained muscle from wrestling daily with the machines and heavy bolts of cloth. He had also acquired a ring of fat around his belly, a combination of Ann's delicious cooking, a slowing metabolism, and a few pints of beer he allowed himself each weekend. As the silhouettes grew smaller before being swallowed up by the early morning fog, she recalled the day James was born. That seems like only a minute ago now. As he grew older, there were the picnics down by the river and on gloomy days after Joshua left for work, they would slip back into bed and snuggle as she told him stories of when she was a young girl. A tear trickled down her cheek as she made a mental note that she should no longer refer to them as "the boys" or "her boys". Instead, she would call them "her men". Joshua was a great father, but it took a few years after they were married to make the transition from being a thirty-plus-year-old bachelor to a husband and family man.

"I'll talk to Chuck, the foreman, when we get there and ask

if it's alright for you to look around through the day so you can see the whole operation. You'll be able to see everything from where the bales of cotton are unloaded at the canal barge, the process through the mill, and as the bolts of cloth are shipped out," Joshua explained as they walked. "He may even show you around some himself if he has time. He's done it for a few others who were interested in mill work."

At lunchtime, James was waiting for Joshua under the lunch shed. "What do you think so far?" Joshua asked as he sat down at the table and began shuffling through the various lunch items.

"I've spent most of the time out at the docks watching the unloading of the bales of cotton and loading of bolts of finished cloth for shipment," replied James. "I found the coal burning and steam engine part real interesting. This afternoon I'll spend most of the time watching the spinning and weaving operations."

That evening, Ann wanted to hear about James' day, but also realized he would be more talkative after he'd eaten and rested a bit. "I'm anxious to hear about your day," Ann finally said, as they licked up the last of a pot of stew she'd been working on all day. Joshua perked up as well, interested in how James would report the day's activities.

I met a lot of the men. Chuck, the foreman, was real nice and gave me freedom to roam anywhere in the mill I wanted. I spent a little time in each area of the mill, from the docks where the bales of cotton came in, to the dock where the cloth left. The steam engine machinery was impressive. Oh, I also saw them unloading a coal barge to fire the steam engine. The looms were noisy. I couldn't believe how loud it was in there and that men work all day every day in that noise," James explained.

"I usually wad up some of the cotton fibers and stuff them in my ears to cut down on the noise," Joshua added.

"What about the spinning floor? You didn't mention anything about that," Ann questioned, anxious to hear what he thought of her former profession.

"Oh, I spent time on the spinning floor too," James explained. "That was fascinating, but it was all women except the floor boss. I guess because of that, I didn't feel too comfortable there and didn't stay long. You could say I saw the whole operation, from coal to cotton to cloth." They all chuckled at his wise-crack. Just then there was a knock at the door. "I'll see who it is," said James as he slid back his chair and went to the door. "Bob? Come on in. We're just finishing dinner."

Since the mumblety-peg days, James had only seen Bob sporadically. When they did cross paths, it was usually competitive. They had moved from mumblety-peg to a more challenging game played by older boys, but it still involved two favorite elements, knives and insults. In this game, the players would find a tree one or two feet in diameter. They would start about ten feet away from the tree and throw the knife so it would stick point first in the tree. If both boys were successful, they would move back a step and try it again. At each new distance, the first boy who didn't stick his knife lost. The creativity of the insults was as much a part of the game as the knife throwing. There were rules there too. On James insistence, the insults could not include any swearing or vulgar references. Bob was often frustrated since his normal conversation was saturated with crude talk. On several occasions in the middle of a game when Bob wasn't keeping the rules, James would just turn and walk away. As he walked away, he would say something like, "Talk like that just shows how dumb you are. Can't you think of anything intelligent to say?" But tonight was different. Bob was out of breath and had something on his mind.

"I've been working up at the mine the last few weeks. Earlier today one of the doormen stumbled and took a bad fall," Bob explained. Now he had everyone's attention and they urged him to continue. "It turns out he'll be alright. He's bruised up some and has a severely sprained ankle. But they need someone in the morning to take his place for a few days until he's back to work. I knew James was looking and thought he might be interested."

They were all surprised by the sudden opportunity. Each looked from face to face trying to read what the others were thinking. "They'll pay doorman's wages. It's on the low end of the pay scale, but it's better than nothing, plus it'll give James an idea of what mine work is like."

Joshua scratched his head, looked at James, then looked at Ann. In turn, Ann looked at Joshua then looked at James and with a worried look asked, "What does a doorman do?"

"It's simple," Bob explained. "You just watch for loaded carts to come down the track and when they do, open the door so they don't have to stop, then close the door behind it."

Little Sarah was sitting on James lap quietly amused by this visitor and the conversation which enlivened the evening.

"Why don't they just leave the doors open all day?" Ann

asked.

Bob lit up as he realized what was obvious to him was not obvious to someone unfamiliar with mining. "The door needs to be closed so air is pushed down the shaft for ventilation. When the door is open, the air escapes instead of being pushed down to the miners."

Again, there was a pause and each looked at the others for some additional input. Finally, Ann said hesitantly, "It's up to you, James. If that's something you'd like to try, then it's OK with me.

She looked over at Joshua, encouraging him to give his thoughts, but he just nodded his approval.

"Sure, I'll give it a try," James finally said.

"Great," Bob said. "I'll be out on the road at six 'o clock, and we can walk to the mine together."

"Six!" cringed James.

Joshua chuckled, then added, "If you are going to become a working man, your sleeping-in days are now few and far between."

CHAPTER

22

The next morning Bob was kicking rocks on the road in front of James' house a little before six o clock. There were streaks of light through the clouds hovering over the eastern horizon, but the sunrise was still nearly an hour away. The early hour didn't dampen Bob's excitement of having James walk along with him. He talked non-stop about the details of the mining operation and particularly the opening and closing of the door, at least from his limited perspective. Bob was also a doorman, but at a different tunnel. They would have no interaction during the day except during the lunch break. Bob wanted to be sure James was aware of all the finer points of the door operation. James was also surprised at how complicated Bob could make such a simple process.

At lunch, Bob was excited to hear every detail of James' morning. Growing tired of Bob's pressing for minute details, he finally said, "The whole morning was basically like you said. You watch and listen for a cart coming down the track, you open the door, let it pass through, then close the door. Oh, and if it feels right, you sneeze while the door is open."

James continued eating his lunch without missing a beat. He didn't look up, but he could feel Bob's face growing contorted with puzzlement as he tried to make sense of James' last comment. Finally, James looked up at Bob, enjoyed the discombobulated look on his face, then smirked ever so slightly. Bob saw the grin and broke out laughing, shaking his head. Nothing else was said during lunch.

At the end of the shift, the miner's routine was to follow the last cart out. James heard them coming and prepared to open the door. They were still about 100 feet down the track, when there were a couple of loud thuds, a man screamed in pain, followed by yelling and shouting of directions overlapped with every kind of cursing. The commotion continued for about a minute, then someone yelled, "Hey doorman, open the door."

James complied. His door was the nearest door to the mouth of the mine. Opening the door allowed some additional light down the tunnel. James could now see the full coal cart with a dozen or more men pacing around it. He could see they were very worked up about something and caught a glimpse of a man lying on the ground who appeared to be partially under the coal cart. James couldn't stop himself from walking towards the tumult. As he got closer, he could see the man on the ground was not only caught under the car, but his leg was under the wheel of the cart. The men were crowding around the car and were trying frantically to lift the cart. A loaded cart would weigh several tons. Unaided men would not be able to lift it.

James slowly walked closer. He noticed out of the corner of his eye, a long, discarded timber that had been forgotten while adding some shoring to the tunnel ceiling. He had an idea, an idea that Joshua had shown him when they were trying to roll a large tree stump out of their yard. Perhaps they could use the timber to lift the cart off the man's leg. He grabbed the timber and dragged it towards the mishap. As he approached, one of the miners said in a disgusted tone, "What are you going to do with that?"

"Two of you roll that rock over in front of the cart," James said calmly but firmly.

The men stared at him briefly, then one said, shrugging his shoulders, "Let's give it a try." Meanwhile, the injured man had passed out from the pain but was bleeding profusely. The miners placed the rock in the spot James had pointed out. He positioned the timber with the short end under the cart and the long end reaching up to the top of the tunnel.

"Put four men hanging on the timber, out as close to the end as possible. Lift them up to it if they can't reach it. The rest of you lift the cart as before."

The men hustled to follow James instructions. As soon as all the men were in place and lifting, the cart rose several inches off the man's leg. James pulled him out from under the cart just before it fell back onto the tracks with a loud thud. With the man out from under the wheel, the bleeding was even worse. James immediately pulled his belt off, made a tourniquet and put it on the man's leg to stop the bleeding.

"Go to the office," the foreman shouted to one of the men. "Tell them we've got a man hurt and need some help. Bring the supply cart down to carry him out on."

After the injured man had been wheeled out, James, the foreman, and a few others were catching their breath as they made their way out of the tunnel. "How did he get his leg caught?" James asked as they walked.

"They were horsing around, and he stumbled on a lump of coal that had fallen off an earlier cart. The full cart rolled up on his leg before we could get it stopped. Who are you?" the foreman asked James. "I haven't seen you here before."

"James Fielding is my name. I'm just filling in today for the doorman who was injured yesterday."

"Lucky for that guy under the cart you were here today. You probably saved his leg, maybe his life. Come back tomorrow. I'll talk to the office. I'm pretty sure there'll be a better job for you here tomorrow," the foreman said as they parted ways.

CHAPTER
23

Bob had missed the hubbub surrounding the incident since he was in a different tunnel at the time, but he heard all about it before he and James met up to walk home together. Bob couldn't stop talking about it and what the foreman might mean when he spoke of a "better job for you tomorrow."

"James saved a man's life today!" Bob blurted out to Ann when they opened the door to James' house.

"What are you talking about?" asked Ann. Bob rattled off the story with all the details without James even opening his mouth. "So, are you going back tomorrow?" continued Ann.

Bob was incredulous, "What are you saying? 'Are you going back tomorrow?' Of course you're going back tomorrow. You've been on the job one day, and they're offering you a promotion." Bob was pacing around the room, arms waving in the air as he spoke.

James and Ann were sitting at the table now. "Let's be realistic," James calmly said. "It doesn't take much of a job improvement to be a step up from doorman. I'll think about it overnight, and if I'm not out on the road at six in the morning, you'll know I decided against it."

Bob rolled his eyes and shook his head as he walked out the door. "Sheesh, I don't believe it," they heard him say.

James had every intention of going to the mine again tomorrow. He was quite interested in what the new job might be. His nonchalance was just an act, but he enjoyed teasing Bob, something left over from the mumblety-peg days. The next morning Bob and James arrived at his front gate about the same time.

"I was afraid you'd gone completely daft and wouldn't show this morning," Bob said when they met.

"To be honest, I am curious what they might offer," James replied.

Bob couldn't quit talking about the possibilities while on the way. When they got to the mine, Bob took his usual spot in his tunnel at the door. James walked to the office. "I'm James Fielding. I was told I should check in here this morning before work," he said to the clerk.

"So, you're James Fielding," replied the clerk, a plain-looking, middle-aged woman. "You caused quite a stir around here yesterday. Have a seat. I'll tell the manager you're here."

A minute later, Fred, the mine manager, came out and greeted James with outstretched hand. "James, glad to meet you. Come in my office. We need to talk." Fred led him into his room. Everything was covered with a thick layer of dust. Papers were piled everywhere and gave the impression he was being asked to do much more than he had time. Everything that wasn't a critical item for the day was relegated to a pile to be addressed later. If it never became critical, it was never addressed.

"We're glad you happened to be filling in yesterday. You probably saved that man's leg and possibly his life," said Fred. James gave a slight nod in acknowledgment of the compliment. "What that incident showed us is you've got a clear head and some common sense, something we don't have enough of around here. Have you had any experience with equipment, you know, machinery?"

James slowly shook his head, searching through his memory for something even vaguely related he could report. He finally remembered something. "A few times I went with my Uncle John out to the farm he worked at and helped him stack hay with a derrick."

"A derrick?" questioned Fred. "Is that the apparatus where ropes and pulleys boost hay up onto a pile?"

"That's right, sir," James replied.

"Great! That's just the kind of experience I'm looking for," said Fred. James couldn't imagine what the connection could be. This was not a farm, but a coal mine. "We need a hoist operator," continued Fred.

"Could you explain, sir?" James was puzzled.

"You use a hoist to raise buckets of coal 200 feet up a vertical shaft from a tunnel down below. Then dump the coal in a bin to be loaded on wagons or barges for shipment," Fred explained.

"It sounds complicated, Sir. I'm sure I've never done anything like that," James said.

"You'll have to be trained," said Fred. "We'll train you. Once you get onto it, it's boring as heck. But it pays well if you can do it. Once you show us you're competent, it pays 10 shillings a week."

James almost choked at the pay rate. He knew Bob was only making three shillings a week as a doorman. James tried to restrain himself and act as if he was having a hard time deciding whether to take the job. Finally, he casually said, "I'll give it a try."

"Good," Fred looked relieved. "The clerk will give you directions where the hoist is. Spend the morning just watching. Watch carefully. There are several critical things you need to know not to tear it apart. Then there are a bunch of finer points, tricks of the trade, that'll boost your production. After lunch, get in the operator's seat and let him coach you to get you up to speed. The bucket hoist is the bottleneck of this whole operation. Piles of coal stack up down below. How much gets put on wagons and barges determines how much income we have each month. And to make a profit, we must be pushing to peak volume every month. That's one reason it pays so well. Welcome to the company," said Fred as he extended his hand again to James.

James' head was swimming at everything he'd just heard and tried to accept the idea that he was going to learn how to run a hoist in a major mining operation. He left Fred's office and approached the clerk, "You're supposed to show me where the bucket operation is," James said to Mary.

"Before I show you, I need some more information. I need your name, birth date, and where you live," she said pleasantly, eyeing James over thoroughly. After James had given her the information, they walked out onto the step where the Mary pointed to a tower several hundred yards away. "That's the hoist tower over there. Walk past the lunch building, past the water tower to your right and up the steps to the tower. I hope you like it here. By the way, my name is Mary, Mary Henthorn," she said calmly. "If you have any questions, or your pay isn't right, see me," shaking James' hand again, firmly and for what seemed to James, a long time.

James followed Mary's directions, but as soon as he was out of sight of the office, he had to stop. He was overwhelmed at what had happened the last few minutes. There was something else. He had never met Mary before, but there was something about her that kept nagging him. "Mary, Mary Henthorn," he thought. "That's it, Henthorn." That's what kept bugging him. Where had he heard that name before?

CHAPTER

24

B ob was comical when James told him what position he had been offered and kept pressing him for how much it paid, but James refused to say. "A little more than doorman," was all James said. "Besides, it depends on whether I can do the job. I may not be able to handle it."

"Don't tell me what it pays," Bob fumed. "I'll ask around. I can find out what a hoist operator makes. Sheesh! I ask you to fill in as a favor to you, and you end up making twice the money I make. The world is so unfair."

"I may not measure up," James tried to calm him down. "No sense saying anything yet when I'm not sure I can even do the job."

"Miss Ann!" Bob shouted as he barged into James' house when they arrived. Bob had got into the habit of calling Ann "Miss Ann", Miss Ann because he felt it reflected his respect James's mum, plus the notion that Ann ruled the home. It didn't take long for anyone familiar with the Hardy home, to realize Ann had ways of achieving the outcome she desired. Joshua, with all his acquired macho, melted when Ann wanted things her way. Ann rather liked the title and Joshua and James tolerated it. "Can you believe it? They're making James a hoist operator and

133

paying him twice what I'm making." Bob tended to get a little carried away when he was on a rant.[5]

Miss Ann gave James a puzzled look, "Is that right James? What's going on?"

"It all depends on if I can even do the job," James said, trying to calm things down a little.

"He spent the day up in the operator's box! He was even at the controls part of the day," Bob continued. Miss Ann looked at James, expecting some clarification.

"He exaggerates," James downplayed. "Late in the day, I did make three bucket lifts to get a feel for the controls. I'm supposed to practice tomorrow with an empty bucket while the operator is eating lunch. Then we'll see."

Miss Ann smiled and shook her head with a pleased look on her face, "At twice the pay?"

"No, not twice," James said while thinking, 'more than three times!' "It all depends on if I can do the job. Let's not get too excited before we know."

Bob stomped out the door, shouting over his shoulder, "See you in the morning." He didn't want to show it, but Bob was quite proud of James. Miss Ann and Joshua were as well.

"Well, I guess this ends your interest at the cotton mill," Miss Ann commented at dinner that evening.

"I've not decided anything yet. We'll see how the next few days go; then I'll decide," said James.

"When it comes to the working man, there are two types," Joshua began philosophically, "The workhorse and the buggy horse." The others knew there was more coming, and waited. "The workhorse gets along best with a pick ax and shovel and is good at pounding away or digging day after day. The buggy horse, on the other hand, can interpret the signals and verbal coaxing from a driver and is better with the details of pulling a buggy or wagon. Both jobs, any job, will be boring and tedious. It comes down to what you'd rather be doing while you're bored."

After a week of spending most of each day watching the lifting operation, getting in more practice time, and increasing the amount of time he was bucketing coal, Fred sent word out for him to come to the office.

"How would you feel about having a shift of your own?" Fred got right to the point.

James felt apprehensive about it. He was controlling a lot of power. There was the opportunity for disaster should he misread the sound of the cables humming, the pressure on the levers, or operate the levers in the wrong order.

"I feel like I'm still getting used to it, sir. I am getting better at it. The first few days I spilled a lot of coal that had to be cleaned up by hand. I know that's not acceptable." James was hedging on his ability and wasn't fully confident he could do an adequate job yet.

"I've seen worse by men who've been at it for months. The regular operator must take the next 4 or 5 days off, maybe longer, starting tomorrow. His wife just had a baby. Neither of them are doing well at all. They may not make it. Be here in the morning

135

at seven. We'll see how you do with a full shift."

James slept poorly that night. In fact, he hardly slept at all. The next morning, as he was going out the door, Miss Ann stopped him. "Wait a second, James." He stopped and turned, giving her a puzzled look. Miss Ann walked over, put her arms around him in a big, extended bear hug. "You can do this, James," she said. "You may make a few mistakes. Fred knows you're new and are still learning the job. He expects you to make a few mistakes. Just keep your head focused on the job and keep at it. Before you know it, the shift will be over. You'll be a better operator at the end of the day than at the beginning, and I'll have something special waiting for your dinner." Miss Ann was getting teary, and so was James.

"Thanks, Mum," he said as he bolted out the door so she wouldn't see the tears in his eyes. Bob was waiting on the road. It was still dark enough so James wasn't worried that Bob might see the tears.

"It's a big day for you, ain't it, James," Bob said as they started walking towards the mine.

"I'm as nervous as a long-tailed cat in a room full of rocking chairs," James answered softly.

"You can do it. I've got confidence in you. Just keep thinking about the big money you'll make," suggested Bob.

"I've thought about that," James replied. "But I think a better approach would be just to concentrate on making the operation as efficient as possible, keep looking for ways to shave even a fraction of a second off each cycle. That'll keep my mind on the operation in a good way."

As James climbed the ladder to the operator's chair, sat down and looked over the levers, cables, pulleys and large bucket he would spend the day controlling, he was visibly shaking. He couldn't believe he, a fourteen-year-old boy, was being given a chance to operate the most critical machine in the whole mining operation. During the first cycle, he almost passed out from hyperventilation. He stopped for a few seconds after he dumped the bucket and let these thoughts run through his head; *"I've made it through a cycle and didn't kill anybody, didn't spill the whole bucket load on the ground and didn't destroy the machine. I just have to pick up a little speed and do the same thing the rest of the day."*

After a couple of hours, he saw Fred standing away off from the operation watching him. He suddenly got nervous again, especially when Fred started walking up to the operator's cab. Fred climbed the ladder to the cab, poked his head in and only said, "You're doing OK. I've been watching you for about 20 minutes, and you're doing OK. When something goes wrong, and it will go wrong, try something, anything. What you try may not fix it, but you'll gradually learn what works and what doesn't." He then climbed back down the ladder and left. That was the only time James ever saw Fred out at the hoisting operation, but it gave him a real boost of confidence.

By the end of the shift, his energy was spent, and he could barely walk home. Working under the stress of the new job gobbled up his strength and left him as limp as a stale carrot. Walking home that day, he said next to nothing to Bob's non-stop questions and comments. Dinner was the same except his parents understood his frame of mind and exhaustion and stopped asking questions after the first one or two. His mother had taught him, "One attribute prized by any employer is absolute, day after day, dependability. Ability is second."

James appreciated the hot apple pie Miss Ann had baked for the "something special" she had mentioned that morning. James went to bed immediately after supper, sleeping soundly all night.

CHAPTER
25

❝ Somebody get James. Maybe he'll know what to do," the shift foreman yelled to nobody particular. A dozen miners were frantic in their efforts to retrieve one of their crew who had fallen into a hole that suddenly opened up in the tunnel where they were working. Everyone was staying several yards back from the hole, not sure how stable the ground was near the edge. Since James had helped save the miner whose leg had become pinned under a coal cart, he had become known for his aptitude and resourcefulness when it came to dealing with pulleys, levers, and machines in general. Others in the company often asked James for his opinion and insight when faced with an unusual or sticky problem.

For over two years, James had been operating one of the company's two hoisting operations, lifting thousands of tons of coal from the tunnel below to the above ground loading facilities for shipment. As the industrial revolution continued to evolve, the cotton mills installed more steam driven machinery, requiring more coal to feed the fires of the steam engines. James' production as a hoist operator improved. Visitors to the mine and even other miners enjoyed watching James operate his bucket. His operation was so smooth and seamless. It never stopped or even slowed down as one phase of the cycle flowed into the next.

"Jonny! Jonny, can you hear me?" the foreman yelled as loud as he could. No response. "I'm going to crawl out on my belly to look over the edge to see what we're dealing with. I want two men, the two heaviest men, one holding each foot, holding me back in case the ground gives away. Someone go to the office and sound the 'ALL STOP' to shut the mine down and bring back Fred and the engineer. Get a good hold, men, or we may have two men down that hole."

The foreman laid flat on the ground. Two men sat, each holding an ankle of the foreman. He inched his way towards the hole. It took over a minute for him to reach the edge. As he peered over the edge, he saw nothing but black. The hole could be as little as four or five feet deep, and he wouldn't be able to see the bottom in the dim light supplied by a torch in the tunnel, or it could be several hundred feet deep. "Hand me the light, so I can see what we're dealing with." He was handed the torch. At first, it was no help. He couldn't see the bottom of the hole or Jonny, the miner who had fallen in the hole. Then when he reached over the edge and lowered the torch as low as he could and let his eyes adjust, he could barely see Jonny's twisted body with arms and legs sticking out at unnatural angles, about 40 feet below on a ledge. He couldn't see how deep it was past the ledge.

Jonathan, or Jonny, as he was called by his fellow miners, was 47 years old. He was an old-timer as far as miners go. Spending all day, every day, underground in the coal-dust-laden mine shaft was brutal for everyone. He was noticeably slower and less productive than most of the crew, which were ten to thirty years younger. He had lived through many mishaps and mine accidents, which gave him a perspective the company deemed valuable. He often buddied up to the young, new hires and freely gave advice and cautions to anyone joining the mining crew.

"Jonny, can you hear me?" shouted the foremen. This time, Jonny responded with a weak grown. There were a few seconds of silence, then a loud groan and scream as the pain began to register. "Lie still, Jonny. We're working to get you out."

"I'm pretty broke up," Jonny managed to say thru clenched teeth. "And my head is bleeding, bad!"

James came running up from the mouth of the tunnel but stopped short when he saw the hole in the ground. "Pull me back," said the foreman when he realized James was there. The two men started heaving him back slowly, careful not to knock any rocks or dirt down the hole.

"James, the floor just gave way and Jonny, one of my men, is about 40 feet down that hole on a ledge. He has at least a broken leg and arm that I can see, and is bleeding badly from a gash in his head. I don't know how stable the ground is around the hole so I wouldn't use anything near the hole as a brace if we can help it."

James nodded his understanding and added, "Let me look it over."

"Everyone, clear the area. Stand back behind that shoring," the foreman yelled, pointing to a twelve-inch-thick timber jammed in the side of the tunnel to shore up the tunnel ceiling. The men cleared the area, and James looked over the situation by the light of another torch that was brought in.

Fred and engineer came running in. The foreman repeated

the same information he'd given to James.

The engineer began assessing the situation and offered an explanation for the cave-in. "There's an old tunnel that runs about 120 feet below this tunnel. We calculated that was enough distance not to jeopardize this tunnel. There must have been a weak fissure in the rock we were unaware of which allowed the cave-in."

James and the engineer were now the only ones left near the cave-in. The rest of the men were standing back, waiting for instructions on what to do next. Fred was talking in low tones to several of the men, asking questions as to the chain of events. He had shifted into management mode and was building a scenario of what had taken place, what had been done, what could have been done and what should have been done. None of which concerned James or the engineer.

"What do you think of this idea," James started to explain, "See that vertical shoring timber against the wall on the other side of the cave-in?" The engineer nodded. "And there is another one on this side of the cave-in." Again, the engineer acknowledged. "Let's bring in a long timber, say a six by eight-inch size, but you can determine what size we need, fix it between the two shoring timbers across the cave-in near the ceiling. Before we put the cross timber in place, we attach a block and tackle with a rope already in it. After it's up in place, we use it to lower a man down to Jonny, have the man tie Jonny to the rope and pull him up. That means the rescuer must stay down there until we can bring Jonny up, untie him and lower the ropes back down to lift the rescue man. What do you think?"

Just then Jonny down on the ledge, called out in a weak voice, "Anybody still there? I can't see anybody." His call was not only weaker but scratchy and stressed. "I can't hold out much longer," his voice trailed off.

"Hang on, Jonny," James responded. "We're getting a plan organized, but it will take a few minutes to put it in place and get it rigged up. We've got Fred and the engineer here working on it as well, and the rest of the crew standing by."

The engineer felt pressed to decide without reviewing all the calculations and "what ifs" as he was trained. He quickly said, "Make the cross timber a four by 12-inch instead of a six by 8-inch," then added after seeing James' puzzled look as to why, "less weight to carry in and about the same strength."

James ran to Fred and rattled off a list of items. Fred, in turn divided up the list between several men. "We'd also better get a doctor on the way and a stretcher and the company nurse down here," James added. Once the plan was in place, things started happening quickly. James edged up to the cave-in and hollered out to Jonny, "Jonny, we've got a plan to lower a man down to you. He'll untie himself from the rope then tie that rope on you. When you're tied on, we'll bring you up. We've called for a doctor to be here when we get you up here. You might see some activity. We'll be careful and try not to knock any dirt and rock loose as we put the pulley in place."

A weak, "OK," was all Jonny could muster as he gave into the intense pain and the loss of blood became critical.

A group of men hurried into the tunnel, four carrying the timber to be used as the cross piece, two carrying the block and tackle and a long rope, and two more with a brace and bit, hammer and spikes to attach the cross piece to the vertical shoring. A block and tackle is a pulley and rope system that would be attached to the center of the cross timber and used to lower the rescue man down to Jonny, then bring Jonny back up. The miners moved quickly and efficiently, preparing for the rescue. They were all quite familiar with handling these tools and materials since they would often install shoring and bracing in the tunnels as they worked their way deeper into a coal vein.

Even though the men moved as quickly as they could, the minutes were mounting. "Jonny? Jonny, can you hear me!" James hollered down to the man on the ledge, trying to keep him conscious and encourage him.

"I'm afraid I won't make it," Jonny weakly responded. "I can't hang on any longer."

"Jonny, don't give up." James continued. "We're harnessing a man on now to lower him down to you." But there was no response from Jonny. James hadn't thought of who they would send down. It wasn't his place to make that decision. He turned to the foreman, "Who do you want to send down?"

The foreman was silent. He had not anticipated having to pick someone to perform the rescue, from which he may not return. The ground was unstable. Additional cave-ins could occur. Plus, there was the added pressure of having to untie himself from the rope, leaving him exposed to falling further down the shaft, and manage to tie on a helpless, probably unconscious man. The foreman decided, with the risks so great, he couldn't ask that of another man. "We need a man to volunteer to be lowered down to help Jonny. It'll be dangerous. I won't lie to you."

Each man in the crew stared at the ground, some in contemplation of the task before them while asking themselves if they were they willing to risk their lives, some in fear. Seconds were ticking by as Jonny's chance of survival diminished. "Men!" shouted the foreman, "will one of you go down?"

"I will, sir," came a voice from behind the foreman. The foreman turned and stepped to the side to let more light into the tunnel to see who was talking. It was James.

"James, you can't…." started the foreman.

"It makes sense," James said cutting him off. "I'm not married. I have no children." Then after a pause, he added to try and brighten the atmosphere a little, "besides, the men have been complaining I eat more than my share when someone brings extra food. Now help me get tied on," as he grabbed the end of the rope and started wrapping it around himself.

Just before they started lowering him down, several men came in carrying a stretcher. The local doctor, Doc Philips, and company nurse, Miss Stein, arrived. "Give him some of this if he's still conscious," Doc Philips said to James handing him a canteen. "It's a mixture of water and laudanum. It'll ease the pain some."

"Put the canteen on your belt and hold the torch in one hand, leaving the other hand free to help maneuver on the way down," said the foreman. "I want six men on the end of the rope. I don't want any slip-ups. Move him nice and slow."

The rope tightened and lifted James off the ground. He

swung out over the cave-in. James caught his breath as he looked down into the black, cavernous hole. He could see no bottom. As he was slowly lowered down into the gaping jaws of unknown darkness, he couldn't help but think, *"What am I doing here? I'd much rather be playing mumblety-peg out by the river, or eating some of Mum's strawberry rhubarb pie. Growing up is no fun."*

CHAPTER

26

Once James was below the rim of the hole, the situation became even more tense. His view of the crew was blocked, as was the sound of conversation. Even though he was only 50 feet from a group of people, he felt utterly alone. A strange feeling. It reinforced the knowledge that the success of Jonny's rescue was up to him. He felt overwhelmed at what he was doing. He would much rather be by the river trading insults and jabs with the other boys from the neighborhood or exploring the woods and hills surrounding his home. Even after running the bucket hoist for several months, he found he had a knot in the pit of his stomach every morning walking to work. The equipment was massive, and there was ample opportunity for disaster. After an hour or two to settle his nerves, he would marvel at what he was doing and the trust the company had in him. At least his work was above ground, elevated above the rest of the mining operation and equipment, able to enjoy the sun, rain, and the wind while Bob and most of the miners worked day after day in the dimly lit tunnels far below.

As James was lowered a few more feet, he moved the torch around to eliminate as best he could, any shadow that would obstruct the light. Jonny's crumpled body came into view. "Something's not right. I'm not seeing him right. That can't be how Jonny is." James blinked hard and shook his head, then looked again. He gasped and swore at what he saw. James rarely swore. Around the miners, it was one of the traits he was known, but no one would admit it. "Jonny! Jonny!" James shouted. Jonny could only groan. What James saw was a leg that was not only fractured but had a compound fracture. The jagged end of the broken bone was sticking through the skin and had even torn through the cloth of his trouser leg. Between the knee and ankle, his leg made a right angle, forward! The other leg was dislocated completely from the socket and was lying next to his back over his shoulder blade. It appeared one arm was reasonably in tack. But the other arm was bent, not only at the elbow but again between his shoulder and elbow. Blood from the gash on his head had drenched his shirt and pants and had formed a pool around his body.

James turned away and vomited at the sight. He felt light-headed. "How am I going to do this? I can barely maintain my composure, let alone help Jonny," he thought. "But I have to. There's nobody else here. If it's going to happen, I have to do it."

"Five more feet then stop," James shouted to the men above. "I'm going to get myself swinging to get over to him.

"How is Jonny," shouted Fred.

"Not good," is all James could say.

The men on the rope and Fred were operating with no view of James. They didn't dare get that close to the edge of the hole, lest they cause some dirt to slough off and fall on the men below. James swung his legs back and forth to get himself swinging until he could grab ahold of the ledge where Jonny lay. He took several deep breaths and looked for a crack he could jam the torch into so he could work with both hands. Accomplishing that, he kicked off several loose rocks from the ledge, so he had a clear space to stand and work.

"What's going on down there?" shouted Fred, alarmed at the noise of the crashing rocks.

"I was just clearing away some of the rubble so I can stand," replied James. "It takes one and a half seconds between dropping a rock and hearing it crash down below. Ask the engineer how far that is." He then turned his attention to how he was going to get Jonny harnessed into the rope so he could be lifted. James had to be sure he was secure on the ledge so he wouldn't slip off while working with Jonny. When he felt like he had a plan, James hollered to the crew above, "Give me ten more feet of rope." James reached into his pocket and pulled out his knife and cut the rope ten feet up. As he did so, he froze with fear, realizing he was untethered as he transferred the rope to Jonny. If he slipped or tripped, he would fall to his death. He tied a large knot in the end, found a crack in the rocks high up on the wall and jammed the knot into the crack as hard as he could. He even found a rock and pounded the knot deep into the crack. Now he felt at least a small amount of security.

"What are you doing?" yelled the foreman.

"Just trying to tie myself off in case I slip," replied James. He then worked the rope behind Jonny and through his crotch, being careful his private parts were not pinched by the ropes. "This will be a story to tell my kids if I ever have any," he muttered to Jonny.

James was surprised when Jonny weakly responded, "I bet

you have a dozen."

"Can you drink some water before we lift you up?" James said softly.

"Water would be good about now. Whiskey would be better," Jonny said.

"Water is all I've got, but the Doc put something in it to help the pain," replied James, pulling the canteen from his belt and putting it to Jonny's lips. He was anxious for Jonny to drink a lot to help the pain, but he had to be careful not to choke him with too much, too fast. Jonny managed to swallow most of the canteen, then shook his head that he'd had enough. In a few seconds, he passed out again.

"That's good," muttered James. "This is going to be unbelievably painful." To the crew up top, he yelled, "I think we're ready. Take up the slack, then hold while I check it over one more time." The crew did as instructed. James double checked his knots and routing of the rope around Jonny's body. Again, to the crew up top, "When you lift Jonny off the ledge, he'll swing a lot. Hold, and I'll try to stop the swinging. Continue when I give the signal."

Jonny let out a moan as his broken leg straightened due to gravity, and his dislocated leg swung 180 degrees from straight up to straight down. James cringed as he knew how painful this was, thankful Jonny was unconscious.

"Haul him up," shouted James as the swinging subsided after a few seconds. Breathing hard from manhandling Jonny's 200-pound body to the right position for the lift, James settled onto the ledge to wait for the rope to be returned.

As Jonny neared the top, one of the miners with a pole and a nail hammered part way in, reached out, snagged Jonny's pant leg and pulled him over to solid ground as he was let down directly onto the stretcher. The doc started immediately assessing his condition. He was barely alive, shallow breaths and feeble pulse. The first thing he did was pull out a needle and thread and sewed up the gash in Jonny's head, stopping the bleeding.

"I've stopped the bleeding but he still may die from loss of blood," the doctor mumbled. Then he looked up and motioned for Fred and the foreman to come closer. "Jonny needs blood immediately if he is going to have a chance of surviving. I've seen it done once a couple of months ago, at a conference."

Both men looked the doc with wide eyes and asked, "You've seen what done?"

The doctor continued, "A blood transfusion." More puzzled looks from all close enough to hear. "I take a syringe of blood, or two or three, from the vein of a healthy man and inject it into Jonny's vein."[6]

There was an audible gasp from the small group of men gathered around. "There is little risk to the person giving the blood," the doctor continued. "He may feel a bit weaker for a few hours after the blood is drawn, but that is all. If we're going to do it, we need to do it now, immediately. Jonny could die any moment."

Fred spoke up, "Is there a man who will volunteer to do this?"

Several seconds passed, then someone asked, "You say there

is little risk to the blood giver?"

"Other than a pin prick in the arm, it's a painless procedure, and it could save Jonny's life," explained the doctor.

"Then I'll do it," came the voice out of the group. The crowd parted, and a young man, covered in coal dust and sweat, stepped forward.

"What's your name," asked Fred.

"Thomas, Sir. Jonny and I are friends. When the ground gave way, I was one step ahead of him in the tunnel. As the ground started collapsing, Jonny gave me a hard push. It was enough to get me onto solid ground. But by pushing me, it pushed him back into the cave-in. That's why he's on that stretcher instead of me."

The doc was already pulling a syringe out of his bag and some alcohol to swab the grime off Thomas' arm for the blood draw.

"It's best if we sit down for this, just so we're both steady during the draw," explained the doc. The doc pulled three syringes full of blood from Thomas and injected them into Jonny's vein. "Now, just lie back and relax for a few minutes before you try to walk and you'll be fine."

After the third syringe, the doc took Jonny's pulse again, then looked up at Fred and smiled. "His pulse is a bit steadier. I think he might make it, but he's got so many other injuries, he'll be laid up for months."

The men lifted the stretcher to take him out just as Mary, the clerk and her daughter came rushing into the tunnel. "Is Jonny dead," the woman frantically asked Fred, nearly fainting when she saw Jonny, pale and bloodied face, lying on the stretcher.

"He's alive for now," Fred replied cautiously. "He wouldn't be if it weren't for James and Thomas," pointing to Thomas seated against the wall on the ground. "We forgot about James!" Fred remembered. "Lower the rope back down and bring James up."

Sitting on the ledge in the dark, James was eager for a chance to sit quietly and catch his breath. He was only able to hear pieces of what was said up top but noted the female voice as Mary and Ann came in and asked questions as to what had happened.

Grabbing the rope as it was lowered back down to him, he tied it around himself and double checked the knot, making sure it was secure and wouldn't slip. "My life depends on that knot," he thought to himself as the rope tightened and lifted him off the ledge. The lift was faster than when he was let down. As he set foot again on solid ground, he looked at Jonny, relieved he was straightened out, covered with a blanket, and the gash in his head stitched up. Several men had lifted the stretcher ready to take Jonny out of the tunnel.

"James, thank-you for saving my Jonny," Mary said as she rushed to him and threw her arms tightly around him, tears streaming down her face.

"Jonny is your husband?" asked James

"That's right. And this is my daughter, Ann," she said pointing to the young woman with her. "She came when she heard there had been an accident in the mine."

"Ann," James said as he nodded. "Ann…Henthorn." Then his

153

eyes grew wide as he swept out the dusty corners of his memory to recall Bob's younger cousin who had followed him to the river several years before. James remembered the girl who was spunky enough to challenge him to a game of mumblety-peg. Her skill at knife-throwing was comical. Nevertheless, James was impressed with her willingness to jump into what was a boy's world.

"Thanks, James, for helping get Pa out of that hole," Ann said as she too threw her arms around James and pulled him tight for a few seconds.

Now the cobwebs cleared from James' mind as he remembered the girl who challenged him years earlier. "WOW! Have you ever grown up!" he almost said out loud, but instead managed to say in a constrained voice, "You're welcome, Ann,"

Most everyone quickly moved towards the entrance, following the stretcher. With most of the commotion gone, James found a place to sit and reflect on the events of the past hour. The mine became quiet. The engineer stayed behind and found a place near James to sit. "Jonny will have a tough road ahead with such severe injuries. If he makes it, he'll be lucky if he can ever work again," the engineer said to James.

"When I first saw him, he was so twisted, I threw up," James admitted to the engineer. "I found myself wishing he would die, so he wouldn't have to be in such pain. When the rope lifted him up, he straightened out a lot. I'm glad he was unconscious. The pain had to be excruciating."

"Not many men could have done what you did today, James," replied the engineer as they stood up to finally exit the mine.

That evening while walking home, Bob respected James' silence, at least for part of the way. "They say you came up with the way to save Jonny today. Is that true, James," Bob asked?

"I suppose so," answered James. "It wasn't anything unusual or complicated."

"I heard the bone had ripped through his skin and his pant leg, and his other leg had been dislocated and was pushed clear back to his should blade. Is that…" Bob started to say, but James cut him off, stopped walking and stared directly at Bob.

"It was the most horrible thing I've ever seen." It'll be months before I can get that picture out of my mind."

"I'm sorry," said Bob. "From what I've heard, it sounded terrible. I won't ask any more about it. I'm glad you're alright. I hope Jonny makes it."

After another 10 minutes of silent walking, James was the one who spoke, "Do you know who showed up in the tunnel after hearing about the accident? Your cousin, Ann. I didn't know Mary, the clerk, was your aunt."

A smile slowly spread over Bob's face as he recalled how James had paid special attention to Ann when she challenged him down by the river, and now James made a point of mentioning her at the mine.

"I may have to pay Jonny a visit in a few weeks and see how he's doing," James concluded as he walked through the gate to his yard.

CHAPTER

27

When James opened his front door and walked in, Miss Ann was right there and grabbed him, wrapping both arms around him. "Thank goodness you're alright," she said, holding him tight and not letting go for a long time. James hung onto to her as well. Finally, they sat at the table. Miss Ann continued, "News of the cave-in and rescue went through the neighborhood like a brush fire."

A few minutes later, Joshua came home from work. A look of relief spread over his face when he saw James sitting at the table. "We're glad you're home. We heard you were in the middle of it." James just nodded his head. "Let's eat, and you can talk about it when you feel like it," concluded Joshua.

Near the end of the meal, James felt he could finally talk about what had happened that day. Details came spilling out as his parents listened silently in amazement. When he finished, Miss Ann said, "What you did today scares me to death, but I'm glad you were there, and they asked for your help. Hopefully, Jonny will recover."

"Tomorrow will probably be just another boring day for you James," Joshua added. "Do you think you can stand that?"

James smiled and shrugged his shoulders, "I hope it's boring."

A couple of months later on a Sunday, James surprised the rest of the family when he said, "I think I'll go over to Jonny Henthorn's and see how he's doing."

"Have you heard anything about how he is recovering?" asked Miss Ann.

"What I hear around the mine is it has been quite painful. He has been miserable. He'll have to stay in bed for several more months, but the pain is a lot better," James replied.

When James walked up to the Henthorn's door, he stood there quietly before knocking. He felt nervous and even a bit sick to his stomach. *"Why should I be nervous?"* he asked himself. *"What's inside this house that I should be nervous about?"* Then he realized that seeing Jonny would bring back the terrible image he had in his mind of Jonny's contorted body lying on that ledge. *"But to see him lying in bed, recovering and in a natural position, would help put that image out of my mind and replace it with a normal one."* He breathed a sigh as he felt part of his anxiety leave.

But there was something else in that house that made him anxious. He was a bit nervous about seeing Ann again. *"Why should I be nervous about that?"* he pondered. Just then, the door opened unexpectedly, and Ann stood before him. For a brief second, he recalled the spunky, freckled-faced girl with pigtails who was bold enough to challenge the older, mumblety-peg champion to defend his title. What stood before him now was breathtaking. She had grown a foot. Her long, combed, brunet hair glistened in the sun. Both were surprised to see the other.

158

A few tortured seconds ensued. Each of them stammering and stuttering to say something intelligent.

Ann finally managed a coherent sentence, "James, what a pleasant surprise. I have been reading to Pa for a couple of hours, and I was just going out for a walk to stretch my legs and get some fresh air. You've come to see him, I presume."

James felt his tongue go numb at the sight of Ann, something that was completely foreign to him. Most of the time, James could rattle off an impressive line of dialogue. A trait that had been honed years earlier by continually trading insults and barbs with Bob and the others as they entertained themselves trying to "one-up" each other. After a little more stammering, he managed to say, "Yes, that's right, uh, that's correct. I am here to see your Pa. How is he doing?"

"Come in and I'll take you to him," invited Ann. "He's doing much better now. The pain has diminished some." Ann led him to the room where Jonny lay, being attended by Mary.

Mary immediately greeted him in glowing terms. "James! Dear James. I'm glad you came. Come in, please." However, Jonny was bewildered by Mary's greeting. He had been unconscious during most of the rescue. He didn't recognize James. Mary, seeing Jonny's puzzlement, explained, "Jonny, James is the one who was lowered down into the cave-in and tied the rope around you so they could bring you up."

"So, you're the one I keep hearing about," Jonny began. "I don't remember much at all during the rescue, except the terrible pain. At times, I was aware of someone talking to me, but I was never alert enough to recognize anyone."

"I could tell the pain was severe," James explained. "Frankly, I'm glad you were unconscious most of the time and missed the worst of the pain," He told Jonny about the blood transfusion procedure. That process left little evidence but was probably equally responsible for Jonny surviving the cave-in. Mary and Ann were also unaware of it. After a few more minutes of visiting, James felt it was time to leave, "I'll stop by again in a few weeks and see how you're doing if that's alright?"

"Thanks for coming by," Jonny said. "I'm lucky I'm here at all. Come again."

"I still need some fresh air," Ann added. "I'll walk out with you, James." When Ann and James were out in front of the house, Ann asked, "Will you walk with me, James."

They walked the first 100 yards in silence. Ann broke the silence, "Thanks for coming by, James. It was thoughtful of you."

"It was good for me to see your Pa in one piece and making a recovery." James continued, "I keep seeing his body, soaked in blood, all mangled, lying on that dark ledge."

Ann, not knowing everything that happened before she and her mother arrived in the tunnel asked, "How did he look before we arrived? And today is the first we'd heard of a blood transfusion. I'm not sure what that is."

James realized he had opened a door that couldn't be closed. It would be hard for Ann and her mother to hear how dire the situation was. He was torn between their desire to know details and wanting to shield them from the stark reality of just how close Jonny came to dying that day. Even Jonny didn't know all the details. He must tell Ann, but he must choose his words carefully.

"I was operating the bucket when the 'ALL STOP' sounded to shut the mine operations down," James started by giving some background. "In a few minutes, a miner came running, yelling that one of the crew foremen wanted me to help solve a problem. I had no idea what had happened or if anyone was hurt. I followed the miner down into the tunnel where the cave-in had occurred. The foreman told me a man was on a ledge about 40 feet below, and they needed a way to rescue him. The engineer soon arrived, and we came up with the plan to rig a rope and pulley to lower a man down, tie the rope on your Pa and bring him up. Everyone could see it was a dangerous plan and whoever was lowered down may not make it back if more tunnel caved in or if he slipped off the ledge." James looked at Ann who was listening intently, trying to process all he was saying.

He continued, "I volunteered to be lowered down because I have no wife or children, so it was best if I did it. When they lowered me down enough to get a good look at him, he was bleeding badly, barely conscious, and his legs and an arm were bent to strange angles. One leg had been dislocated from his hip and was bent back to his shoulder blade. The bone of the other leg was broken and sticking through his pant leg." Ann gasped at the last detail.

James quickly continued so she wouldn't dwell on that image "His shirt was soaked in blood from the gash in his head. By the time you got there, his legs had been straightened out some, and he was on the stretcher with a blanket over him. His bloody shirt had been cut off him to help the doctor assess his injuries."

James stopped talking. He had dumped a load of information on her, and she would need some time before continuing. When Ann felt she could handle more, she asked, "What about the blood transfusion? Tell me about that."

"I didn't see that part because I was waiting on the ledge down the hole. The engineer told me about it. The first thing the Doc did was to quickly sew up the gash in his head to stop further bleeding. He had lost a lot of blood, and Doc said he could die any moment if he didn't get a blood transfusion. The Doc had only seen it done once, and it only helped some of the time. Jonny was close to dying, so it needed to be done immediately. Simply put, they take blood from a healthy man and inject it into a vein of the injured man. There is little risk to the man that gives the blood. Thomas volunteered because, at the moment of the cave-in, Jonny pushed him onto solid ground, but Jonny went down with the cave-in. The Doc took three syringes full of blood from Thomas and put them into your Pa. The Doc said that probably saved his life." Now both were quiet. James noticed Ann wiping away tears that were running down her cheeks. They continued to walk, mostly in silence for another 30 minutes. When they arrive again at Ann's house, they stood in awkward quiet outside the gate.

"Now that Pa is improving and doesn't need constant care, I plan on starting work at a mill in a couple of weeks," Ann said as the moon came over the horizon and the night chill pushed Ann to tighten her shawl.

"Spinning?" questioned James.

"That's right," replied Ann. "I would have started already, but

162

Pa needed someone with him until he improved."

"My mother ran a wheel for about five years spinning one thread at a time before she married my Pa. I understand it's becoming entirely different now with bigger, steam-powered machines," James commented wanting to leave on a brighter topic than Jonny's injuries.

"One person can do what eight people did before. And some mills are installing even bigger machines," Ann explained. "Those who won't or can't learn to run the bigger machines are being fired. It often seems a young, inexperienced person can pick up running the machines better than older workers who have been doing it the same way for most of their lives."

"I hear it's even causing some riots by those who have lost their jobs," James added. "But the steam power is cranking up the demand for coal. Speaking of coal, there's a machine at the mine that will miss me if I'm not there early in the morning. I'd better go, Ann. I enjoyed the visit…especially our walk."

"You've given me, I mean us, a lot of new information tonight. Thanks for coming." Ann looked up at James, then buried her head in his chest, with arms around him, and added, "Please come again."

For the first few minutes walking home, James felt like a limp noodle. His legs would barely carry him. The emotion sucked from his body during the visit left him exhausted. But, as he walked, he found his exhaustion being replaced by excitement, energy, even elation. The horrible image of Jonny, twisted and barely alive, had been replaced by one that was mending and optimistic. In Jonny, he had found a friend with whom he shared one of the most dramatic experiences of their lives. But, more importantly, when he thought of Ann, he wanted to sing. She felt like his soulmate. "But how could I feel that way, I barely know her. I'm getting ahead of myself," he chided. "I'd best put these feelings on the shelf and wait to see what happens."

When James arrived home, he was almost dancing as he entered the house. "How did it go?" asked his mum.

"Fine. Just fine!" James said with a big smile as he bounded up the stairs to his room.

"That's strange," remarked Miss Ann to Joshua. "I don't think I've ever seen James act like that. I wonder what it means?" as she blew out the light for the night, unaware there had been any interaction with a girl named Ann Henthorn.

CHAPTER

28

❝ James, take Sarah for a walk or something," Miss Ann pleaded with James. It was a Sunday, and James was home from work. "She's wrecking my concentration with all her questions. I need to focus on mending your Pa's pants or he'll have nothing to wear to work tomorrow." Six-year-old Sarah was going through a phase where her curiosity triggered a constant, daily barrage of questions. At times, it pushed Miss Ann to the limits of her patience.

"Sure, Mum," answered James. "Come on Sarah. Let's go over the hill to Rooden Lake. From the hill above the lake, you can see our house and all the way to Oldham. Put some bread and cheese in a sack, I'll bring a jug of water, and we'll have a picnic while we're gone."

Sarah squealed in anticipation of the adventure. Miss Ann shot James a look of alarm, "How far is it? It sounds like you're going on quite a trip."

"It's a little more than a mile, over the hill," James said as he pointed in the opposite direction of Oldham. It'll take us the rest of the day, but we'll be home for supper."

"I won't know what to do with that much silence in the

house. Thank you, James."

Sarah scurried around gathering up the items James had mentioned, excited to be going so far from home, and excited to be going with James. Even though there were fourteen years between them, they shared a special bond. In Sarah's eyes, James could do no wrong. He thoroughly enjoyed being the big brother, showing off Sarah to his friends at every opportunity. The hill they were going to climb to get to Rooden Lake rose only 300 feet from their house and was a gradual climb. They stopped often to examine a rock or a butterfly. James reminded himself that the real goal of the hike was not to make the trip to Rooden Lake and back, but to get Sarah out from under the foot of Miss Ann for several hours. To make it all the way to the lake and back would be a bonus.

"Let's see if we can see our house from here," James said when they were about halfway up the slope. He turned around, shielded his eyes, and emitted a few words and grunting sounds designed to impress Sarah. He studied the valley below, stretched out his arm and pointed his finger at some trees in the valley, and for good measure, sighted down his arm and finger as if he were aiming an arrow. "See that bunch of trees and the bright spot where the sun reflects off a stretch of water? That's Beal River."

"Ok," Sarah replied hesitantly. The view from this elevation was a new experience for her. She took her time in looking to the right, the left, near and in the distance, where dozens of smokestacks of Oldham could be seen.

"Follow that line of trees to the left a little to where it crosses a road. That road is Beal Road." James talked slowly, allowing

Sarah time to pick out the objects he mentioned. When he felt Sarah had found the road, he continued, "Follow the road away from us past one, two houses. The third house, the one with the tall pine tree, that's our house."

"Oh," Sarah excitedly said. "I wonder if I can see Pa working in the yard?" She squinted and strained her eyes to help focus."

"He'd be pretty hard to see from this far away," said James.

"What are all those tall sticks in the distance?" Sarah asked, looking at the horizon.

"Those are the smoke stacks at the mills in Oldham, where Pa works," James explained.

"Which one does Pa work at?" Sarah asked.

"I couldn't pick it out from this far away, but it will be one of the closer ones," replied James. Just then a flock of ducks flew overhead in their familiar V formation. They were low enough you could hear their wings beat the air and the occasional quack. "I'll bet those ducks are headed over the hill to the lake. Let go and see if they land." James walked towards the top of the hill, which was another 200 yards further.

As they reached the top of the hill, the lake came into view. Sarah oohed and awed. The lake was quite small, a pond really, only about three acres, but was impressive since it was the first lake Sarah had seen. During the dry part of the year, the lake nearly dries up.[7]

"There are the ducks!" squealed Sarah, pointing to the other side of the lake.

"Let's go sit under that oak tree and eat our picnic," James said pointing to a large oak tree a short way towards the lake. They were both ready for a rest and some food. The shade felt good in the mid-afternoon sun. A gentle breeze added to their comfort. After eating the bread and cheese, James laid down on the ground with his hands behind his head, intending on dozing a few minutes.

"Ewe! Aren't you afraid bugs will crawl on you?" Sarah asked

"Nope. I'll just flick them off if they do," James said nonchalantly. "It does bother me if a grasshopper gets under my shirt. All that kicking and scratching he does trying to get out drives me crazy."

Sarah shivered at the thought, then asked, "Can I ask you a question, James."

"Of course," replied James.

"Do you ever burp? When I burp, Mum gets after me and says it's not ladylike."

"Everyone burps, even Mum," answered James. "The trick is to do it quietly." James emphasized the word "quietly". "This is a real nice spot with the shade from the tree, a view of the lake, and the breeze. I'm going to remember this place and maybe use it in the future."

Sarah was puzzled by that comment. "What are you talking about? It is a nice spot, but..."

James cut her off, didn't answer her question, and instead said, "We'd better start back."

At the top of the hill, James stopped so they could take a long look at the lake on one side and an excellent view of the valley stretching out for nearly 20 miles on the other side. Being Sunday, the usual 300 smoke spewing smokestacks were shut down, giving a clean air view. From where they stood, it was about two miles to Oldham, and James could even make out the outskirts of Manchester which lay about three miles farther.

"This was fun, James," Sarah commented. "Let's see what we can find on the way down," as she took off skipping down the gentle slope.

Miss Ann nearly fainted as the door to the house flew open, followed by a desperate struggle between James and Sarah to see who could get through the door first. James feigned a hurt knee allowing Sarah to race through the door and to her mother's side.

"I beat you, James. I told you I could." Sarah shouted between gulps of air. James plopped down on a chair at the table, looking defeating.

"Calm down you two. You nearly scared me to death," Miss Ann scolded as Sarah joined James at the table. "It sounds like you had a good time."

"From up there, I could see all the way to Oldham where Pa works,"

Sarah said between breaths. "I could see our house and the lake is real nice, and there's a big oak tree we sat under for the shade and had our picnic." James was content to sit quietly and let Sarah have the spotlight. Plus, he was pleased she had enjoyed the adventure.

"Well, while you were gone, I got your Pa's pants mended, and I made a pot of stew. So, get washed up. I'll call your Pa in from the yard and we'll have supper.

CHAPTER

29

Ann Henthorn went to work in a mill shortly after the first visit from James. She became a spinster as well. Instead of spinning one thread at a time, she learned to run a spinning jenny as it was called, spinning eight threads at a time. She became an example of one person doing the work of eight.[8]

"Did you see James today?" she would ask her mother almost every night when she returned home.

"I hardly ever see James," was her mother's response one night after repeated inquiries. "He works hard, is dependable and solves most of his problems himself. About the only time I see him, is when there is a problem with his pay. He is meticulous at watching his pay. He even brought back a half-shilling, which he said he didn't deserve. Now who does that?"

Ann was beaming, just hearing talk about James. Then Mary wrinkled up her brow and looked sideways at her, "Just what do you expect to happen with James?"

"I don't know what will happen," Ann said as she carried some garbage out the back door. "But I know what I want to happen."

"I did see him yesterday, now that I think about it," Mary remembered. "Fred asked to meet with him."

Now Ann was determined to comb out every morsel of information she could about the meeting, "Is he in trouble? Did you hear yelling? Was he frowning or smiling when he left? How long was the meeting? Was Fred mad after the meeting? Did the manager…"

"Stop!" protested Mary. "When James left, he was fine; rather he was preoccupied, looking like he had something on his mind."

"What was it?" Ann was beside herself. "Was it a change in job assignment? Was it a raise? Was it a demotion?"

"I don't know. I just got the feeling it was nothing bad," Mary said as she left the room to stop the barrage of questions.

James did leave the meeting with something on his mind. Fred had explained the demand for coal was excellent. It had been good for several years, driven by increased use in hundreds of mills that were in the area. The mine owners wanted to expand the mine and install another bucket lift. James had been running a bucket now for over five years and was consistently the top producer. Fred wanted James to be the new foreman over the bucket operation. He would have four to six people under his direction and would train new members added to the crew. As James left the office, he was feeling the weight of the added responsibility. The upside was, there would be an increase in his pay. He mulled over the whole scenario as he pulled levers and operated foot pedals to keep the flow of coal moving from the depths below to the loadout bin.

"Am I up to this responsibility?" he thought to himself. *"I've never supervised a group of men before. When I mentioned this to Fred, he pointed out how I organized the rescue of Jonny Henthorn. As I think about it now, something inside me took over and I realized if it was going to happen, I was going to have to do it. A picture of how we should construct the rope and pulley appeared in my mind, and I just acted on it, giving directions on how to carry it out."* James recalled what had happened, several years after the rescue.

Then a thought struck him so forcefully he stopped operating the bucket, *"God put that picture in my mind!"* Then the next thought struck him just as sharply, *"I have not thanked him!"* James stopped running the bucket, something that never happened unless it broke down. He bowed his head and for the first time in his life, had a real conversation with God. A conversation, meaning an exchange of thoughts and feelings. Not only did he express his gratitude to God for helping him see the method of rescue, but in return, he felt confirmation that the actions he took were right. It was a good feeling. He wanted to remember that feeling forever.

A few minutes later, he was interrupted by someone on the barge being loaded, wanting to know what was the problem. "No problem," he shouted back as he again operated the levers. James had gone to church mostly as a pre-teen with Miss Ann and Joshua, but his attendance had become more sporadic as he had gotten older. After today, he promised himself he would attend and pray more often.

Just before quitting time, still thinking about his new responsibility, he was hit with another thought that almost lifted him out of his chair, *"With the pay increase, I can now get serious with Ann."*

CHAPTER

30

66 Mary, is Ann home?" James asked, standing on Ann's front step on a Sunday afternoon. It had been two weeks since James' meeting with the mine manager. The details of the expansion of the bucket operation had been worked out, and construction was underway on building the new bucket and hoist. One other miner had been promoted to Hoist Operator so far to allow James to spend part of his time reviewing and directing the expansion work.

Mary gave James a warm smile as she said, "I've been expecting you for over a week now, James. Come in and sit down. I'll get Ann." James looked sheepish and stared at the floor. When Ann heard her mother welcome James at the door, she jumped and ran to her room to straighten her hair and change into a clean dress. "Ann was helping clean a chicken we killed earlier to have for dinner. She went to clean up and will be here in a few minutes. I understand they've put you in charge of the expanded bucket operation," Mary said while waiting for Ann.

James felt embarrassed and said, "I don't understand it. I have no experience overseeing workers. They say it's because I seem to have the good understanding of machines and how to keeping them running. The good thing is, it will keep me working above ground. Not many men can say they are miners and still work above ground."

Ann came in wearing a clean dress and was all smiles at the presences of James. For a few seconds, they just enjoyed looking at each other. A week earlier James happened to see Ann at the mining office. Mary had forgotten her lunch and Ann had brought it to her. Everyone in the room felt todays visit would become a regular occurrence.

"I thought you might like to go for a walk this afternoon," James suggested. Ann said nothing, but nodded her agreement and started walking toward the door.

"I'll finish cleaning this chicken and get it cooking," Mary injected. "It should be ready to eat about the time you get back. James, please plan on staying for supper."

James was focused on Ann and was oblivious to Mary's invitation, but caught himself just before they closed the door, "I'd love to, Mary."

When they got to the road, James instinctively turned toward the Beal River. They walked along in a bubble which excluded everything and everyone else, basking in a mini celebration of finally arriving at a significant life-point. This journey had started about eight years earlier with an innocent game near the river. Both had matured dramatically, physically and mentally. Ann had long brunette hair, down below her shoulders. Her eyes were blue and clear as if she saw everything in sharp focus. James learned to avoid looking into her eyes. When he did, he turned into putty and found himself mesmerized, unable to speak in coherent sentences. Her figure had developed nicely. A point not lost on James. But perhaps the most striking trait was her openness and ability to speak directly to his soul. There was no pretending she was something she was not. Even though she was only 17, Ann knew what she wanted. She wanted James. She also sensed he may need some time to come to the same conclusion.

James had developed bulging muscles from operating the bucket levers and foot brakes with the precision of a surgeon day after day. By raising, lowering, and dumping the bucket with a constant flow, he squeezed out every pound of coal production he could in a day.[9]

He had blue eyes and blond hair, rather long from only not wanting to take the time to have it cut, but that would change now. A haircut, a good haircut, was near the top of his to-do list. James had learned some basic reading and writing, and composing a to-do list in clumsy block letters was his way of practicing the skill. However, signing one's name was reserved until your writing was mastered. Until then, which often never happened during one's lifetime, an identifying "X" would do.

James was a bright man who moved and talked with confidence that other men, even much older men, respected. James was 20 years old. There were many in the mining crew who were younger, but none younger who had the responsibility he now had.

"Mum has told me about your promotion. I'm intrigued. Please tell me more," Ann asked after a few hundred feet of sauntering down the road.

"I'm quite nervous about it," James began. "I've never overseen a crew before. I'm comfortable with the machinery, but men, I'm not sure about."

"The company wouldn't have asked you if they didn't think you could do it. To me, it looks like the perfect combination of machine knowledge and ability to lead men. You've demonstrated your ability to direct men in a crisis, both with the cave-in and when the miner got trapped under that coal cart. I understand that's different than discussing work schedules or time off. Just remember two basic rules, be honest with them and don't play one against another."

James nodded his agreement. He learned a basic rule that stuck with him throughout his life, "When Ann gives advice, pay attention."

They continued walking, mostly in silence. When they got to the river, James turned off the road and started walking to the familiar mound that had become unique to James and his parents.

"What is this place?" asked Ann, eyeing the well-worn picnic spot complete with a fire pit and scattered, sawed off stumps for people to sit on.

James had been so deep in thought, mulling over his upcoming job duties and Ann's words of advice, he was surprised himself to realize where he had led them. "Oh, this is a favorite picnic spot for our family. We come here a lot during the summer when the house is too hot. The river being close, there is usually a breeze to make the evenings bearable. Now that I think of it, we come here as well in the winter when the weather is good enough just to get out of the house."

They each picked a stump and sat down· "The only bad thing about this spot is sometimes the mosquitos and flies make it a challenge to sit and enjoy the river flowing by and the trees·

Calling the Beal River a "river" was a stretch· Beal Creek would have been more accurate· During the rainy season it was close to a river calling it a creek or brook would have been a better description the rest of the year· It was flowing water and because of that it had been a draw for various groups and activities for decades·

James and Ann sat on the stumps for several hours talking as if they had been saving it all up just for this occasion· Finally when the shadows of the tall trees reached them James realized it wouldn't be long before the sun would set· "We'd better head back before it gets any later· Your mother will be wondering about you" James said as he slowly got up and stretched out his legs·

"She won't be worried·" replied Ann· "But that chicken should be cooked by now and there won't be any left for us if we wait too long·"

When they got back to Beal Road and started towards Ann's home James took a deep breath and took hold of her hand not sure if she'd jerk it away or enjoy it· The touch of her skin felt good to James· She squeezed his hand back indicating she intended to leave it right there· The toughest part of the day the worst part of the day was when James had to leave her to walk home after a friendly and tasty meal with her family· "I'll make it a point not to stay away too long" James said as they parted at the end of a very satisfying day·

CHAPTER
31

The rain was pouring down as James worked the levers on the bucket hoist. It had taken over a year to build the new bucket lift. Everyone called the new, ongoing project the "new bucket", but it was much more than that. There had been new bins built to dump the coal into, which meant there needed to be new docks constructed to load the coal onto barges, and some new roads built so wagons could position themselves for loading. Some mines were starting to use rail to transport their coal, but sufficient track had not been laid to allow general use of the railroads.

The weather had alternated between an annoying drizzle and a torrential downpour every day for the past month. The mining continued underground regardless of the weather, so the bucket lifts had to work. The bucket operator stations had canopies over them to shield them from the rain, but on some days, the cold was intense. It seldom snowed, but the temperature would hover just above freezing for weeks. After a day of bitter cold, wet weather, James would park himself right next to the stove all evening, soaking up as much heat as he could.

"Have you seen Ann lately?" Miss Ann asked one night as he crowded the stove.

"No, I haven't," James replied. "Between the extra time I'm spending getting the new bucket going and the rain, I haven't seen her for nearly a week."

"You like her, don't you?" Miss Ann felt this was the right time to probe James feelings a little.

James nodded and chuckled a little. "I do, Mum. I feel at ease and energized when I'm around her. I know what you're thinking, do I love her?" To that question, he paused as he took an inventory of his feelings, deliberating for a bit while his mother carefully watched his face, trying to interpret what she saw. After what seemed a long time, a smile slowly spread over his face, evolving into a toothy grin, "Yes, I do, Mum. I do love her. There is no one I'd rather be with."

"Just be sure you treat her right," his mother said. Having extracted the information she was after, she concluded, "I'm going to bed."

Verbalizing his feelings to his mother had the effect of cementing James' course of action. He started thinking long term about Ann. He wasn't in a hurry to get married, but he decided he would work towards that goal.

The next day at the mill where Ann worked, as the rain was pouring outside, Ann was being embroiled in a storm inside the mill, not of her doing.[10]

"You can't fire me!" screamed a mill worker who had just been informed she was being fired in anticipation of a new spinning mule being installed. "How will I buy bread and milk for my boy? It's not fair." Then after a pause, "Why don't you keep me on to run the new machine?"

David, the foreman, looked at the floor, took a deep breath and looked up into the face of the distraught woman, "I have my orders. It's not up to me. It's been decided. Ann, Helen, and Jackson will be kept on to run the mule." Unfortunately, Ann, Helen, and Jackson were only a few steps away, witnessing this standoff.

"Why them and not me?" argued the worker. "Ann has no kids, and she's not married. She's even living with her mother, who is a clerk at the mine. I need the job more than she does!"

"It's not a matter of who needs the job the worst," countered David. "It's a matter of who can do the best job. Running a complicated machine like the mule takes a different kind of skill. You need the skill of knowing how a machine works and how to keep it going. It's almost a gift. It seems that younger people more often have this gift. Older folks are used to doing everything by hand." David had crossed the line with his last comment.

"Us 'older folks' haven't got it?" the worker's voice had raised to a screech, attracting the attention of several hundred others who were also being let go. "I'm only twenty-eight. Ann is eighteen. This sounds like a crock of sour milk to me," the women yelled at the top of her lungs. Then she started chanting, "Men, not machines. Men, not machines." Others joined in and crowded around the arguing group. Ann, Helen, and Jackson were being pushed into the chanting, crowding group. All work in the mill had now stopped, and the chanting group grew larger and louder. Ann was frightened. She'd heard about the occasional job riot that had erupted at various mills as machines replaced workers being laid off.

The whole situation was getting unruly, and Ann's eyes darted around the group looking for a way out as she was jostled towards the center of the disturbance. Ann instinctively took a step backward. A few of the shouters stepped around her and now were in front of her. *"That's it,"* she thought to herself. *"I'll just keep stepping backward towards the door as the crowd and those coming through the door are stepping forward."*

Ten steps later she was at the back of the room and quickly backed out through the door, ran down the stairs and out into fresh air. She breathed a sigh of relief and started walking quickly towards home. She wanted to run, but resisted, knowing that would attract unwanted attention. As she left the mill yard, she stopped briefly and looked up at the floor where the ruckus was ongoing. It was even louder now with some people yelling insults and demands. There were several loud crashing sounds. Ann supposed that could be the destruction of some of the machines. *"I'd give her my job if it would stop the riot,"* she thought as she put distance between her and the mill.

Ann hurried home, quickly stepped in and shut the door. When she turned around, Mary was standing at the table fixing supper but became alarmed when she saw Ann, quivering, white as a sheet, and panic in her eyes. "Ann, what's wrong?" Mary said as she stepped close and wrapped her arms around her. She could feel Ann shaking as she started to sob.

"Let's sit down, Mum, before I fall," Ann whispered.

They moved to the table and sat. Ann buried her face in her hands, "It was terrible. There is a riot going on at the mill." Ann paused a few moments to catch her breath. Mary's eyes grew wide, waiting for more information. "Remember I told you the mill is switching over to using spinning mules replacing the jennys they've been using?" Mary just nodded. "They announced today that Jackson, Helen, and I would be running the mules on our floor, and six other workers will be running two other mules that are being installed. They will keep six others as mechanics for the new machines. Everyone else will be laid off." By now, Ann had caught her breath and looked up directly into her mother's eyes. "They're laying off 450 workers and only keeping 15 of us. They tell us that 15 of us will be able to produce more thread than 450!"

"They announced that you're one of the fifteen?" Mary questioned.

"Yes, the protests and arguments started when they said the others would be laid off. It grew until it erupted into a riot. I was caught in the crowd for a while until I saw a way to get out. I was able to slip out and come home. As I left the building, there was terrible noise. It sounded like they were doing damage to the machines. I'm not sure I could go back to work there now."

Mary reached out and held her hands tightly to comfort and reassure her. "You're home now. You're safe. We'll find out in the morning what the outcome is."

CHAPTER

32

❝ Hi Mary, is Ann at home?" James asked. The news of the riot had spread quickly. The next day James went straight to Ann's house after work to find out how she was.

"James, I'm glad you came," replied Mary. "Come in. I'll let her know you're here." James entered and sat down at the table while Mary went into the other room to get Ann.

As Ann came, James stood up and held her tight, finally asking, "How are you, Ann? Tell me what happened." The three of them sat around the table, and Ann recounted the same story as she had told her mother the night before. James had heard most of the details while at work during the day, so he was not surprised. "Have you heard from anyone at the mill today?" he asked.

"No. I've stayed in the house all day, not wanting to be out among people. I'm part of the focus of the riot, but I did nothing to encourage it," Ann said.

James stood and said firmly, "I'll go down there right now and see what I can find out. Nobody knows me there. Don't worry. I won't be gone long."

As James left the house, Ann admired the sight of him, a

tall, broad-shouldered, muscular man who seemed to know what he was about and where he was going. She felt a tinge of pride and a cushion of security, knowing he was her protector. He was intimidated by no man, but humble, knowing he was aware of little of what was going on in the world around him.

James drew close to the mill entrance. He could see a large pile of debris near the mill doors. Coming closer, he could identify pieces of the spinning jennys that had been humming away producing cotton thread just yesterday. A ragged line of six workers continued to carry out machine pieces in the fading light and toss them onto the pile. Another worker was splashing some whale oil on the pile. James approached him as he struck a match, then lit the pile of rubbish.

"They sure made a mess of things, didn't they," James said to the man, giving the impression he already knew some details. In this way, James hoped to extract more particulars.

"What a waste," the man replied as the flames gradually caught hold and grew higher. The man then grunted and continued, "The rioters didn't change anything in the long run. In fact, they probably sped up the changeover."

James now had the man in his confidence and prodded him further, "What do you mean?"

"They've shut the mill down for three maybe four weeks while they clear out the old machines and install the new ones. Those who were to be laid off are out of work now, instead of having another two to four weeks of work while they gradually made the transition. They're asking those who'll be kept on to come in and help with the cleanup and installation of the new machines."

"Was anyone hurt last night?" James asked further.

"There sure was. The Sheriff and about thirty deputies were called in They rounded up about half of the rioters and hauled them off for the destruction of property. When they started doing that, there was a real fight going on, gashed heads, broken arms, broken noses. Nobody killed, yet. A couple of them were in bad shape. It'll take months for them to recover."

James had heard enough. As the flames grew higher, providing enough light for the cleanup work to continue, he thanked the man and strolled off into the dark towards Ann's house.

Ann stood at the table kneading some bread. Mary had asked her to help make several loaves of bread. It provided an outlet for the nervous energy that otherwise would plague her. When she heard James coming up the steps, she flew to the front door, threw it open and looked James over carefully for any injury, then to his face to determine his frame of mind.

"I'm glad you're back. Are you alright? Come, tell us what you found," Ann said as they embraced.

"You were smart not to stick around when the ruckus started," James began. "It got pretty violent. The Sheriff with some deputies came and rounded up about half of them and hauled them off." Ann and Mary's eyes grew wide as they listened to the details. "There were some pretty bad injuries before it was over."

"Was there damage to the machines? What happens now?" asked Mary.

"There was damage. A lot of damage." Ann and Mary were hanging on his every word. "So much so, they're hauling all the jennys out, piling them up and burning them." There was an audible gasp at this last detail. After several seconds of silence, James continued, "They're going to ask those who have been asked to stay on, to help with the clean-up and installation of the new machines."

"I don't know anything about the new machines," Ann protested. "How could I help install them?"

"You'd be a helper to a mechanic," said James. "There will be a lot of drilling holes in the floor and bolting parts together. Easy stuff once they show you what to do. If you feel threatened or unsafe in any way, I don't want you to go. The rioters are still upset at losing their jobs, and they may continue to make trouble."

The next day David, the foreman from the mill, knocked on Ann's door. After being seated at the table and sipping a cup of tea, he began. "I'm sorry how things have turned out. I keep replaying it over in my mind, asking what I could have done differently to avoid what happened. The end results would still be the same, a lot of people out of work. I'm caught in the middle. If the owners can't remain competitive and make a profit, they'll close the mill so even more people will be out of work. I know they've put off modernizing for several years just to keep people working. The modern machines are here to stay. A worker has to learn how to run them, or find another job, or have no job." After another sip of tea, he continued, "I'll get off my soap box. Ann, I'd like you to start coming in day after tomorrow to help install the new mules. Will you do that?"

"Why was I picked to stay on?" asked Ann.

David spoke with ease, enjoying Ann's hospitality, "I've known this was coming for nearly a year now. The owners charged me with observing how everyone worked their jenny and who would most likely be good at running the new machines. The new machines are very different, so the skills from running a jenny won't transfer directly to a mule. What is important is machine sense. The process still starts with cotton fibers and the end product is still thread. How the machine produces thread from the fibers is different than with the jenny. The question is, 'who can produce the same product using a different route'. I've noticed you're not afraid to try different ways to solve a problem you encounter. You're quite resourceful in handling your problems. Everyone who is being asked to stay has this same ability."

"Is it safe? Will the rioters continue to cause trouble?" Ann asked.

David could see the fear in her eyes. "The owners have authorized me to hire five tough guys...uh... I mean, security men to watch out for any troublemakers. It'll be safe, or I'll send you home," he said defiantly. David finished his tea and stood up to leave, "Can I count on you?" he asked.

Of course, she wanted to keep her job. Mills all over Oldham were making similar improvements. She should count herself lucky to be one of the few chosen to stay on, but she dreaded the inevitable times when she'd be in town shopping for food and run into friends and acquaintances she'd known at the mill who hadn't been so lucky and had been fired. What would she say to them? What would they say to her? She was fortunate to be one of those who could learn how to run the new machines, developing skills and knowledge that would keep her in demand.[11]

Ann slowly nodded her head and finally said, "I'll be there."

CHAPTER
33

Ann found she enjoyed learning about installing the new machines with all the different parts and how to assemble them. It took fifty wagons to deliver each mule. The pieces were then organized, laid out on the mill floor, and bolted together. The start-up of each machine took over a week and hundreds of fine adjustments until they reached a consistent, final product.

"How do you like your new job?" James asked several months later. They were spending their Sunday afternoon together as usual. This Sunday, they had walked again to their favorite spot near Beal River. It was early spring and chilly, but that didn't dampen the lure of being able to spend some time together. James had built a fire that day. He had also found a good-sized log, manhandled it next to the fire pit and even hewed off a flat spot on one side to make a nice place where they could sit close together.

"I love the new job," Ann replied enthusiastically. "It has taken a while to get it running smoothly, but now, instead of sitting in one place all day, I walk up and down the mule making little adjustments to keep everything working smoothly. I'm amazed at how much thread just three of us can make. How is the new bucket operating?" The rapid growth in the cotton cloth industry had brought about expansion and modernization in both industries. Being young, bright and eager to learn had benefitted them both in their jobs.

"We finally got the kinks worked out of the new machinery," James replied. "I'm still getting used to scheduling and running a crew. It also means I answer directly to the manager for any problems with the crew. I'm in charge of hiring and training new crew members and firing when needed. I especially don't like that."

"Has that happened often?" asked Ann.

"A couple of times already," explained James. "Not just anybody can run a bucket. It takes a certain talent and ability. Because it pays more than most mine work, there are many who apply for the openings. One man, I had to fire because he," James paused, looking for the right words to explain what he wanted. He finally continued, "Because he was clumsy. He spilled coal everywhere that had to be cleaned up by hand. He was rough on the equipment. I was afraid it would need to be rebuilt before the month was out. The other man I had to let go, showing up for work drunk. For that, there is no tolerance. You not only endanger the equipment, you endanger the other miners."

Sitting close to Ann, staring into the hot coals of the fire, sharing his week with her and hearing about her week, was James' absolute favorite part of the week. Until a few months ago, James refused to think about the word "marriage," but it popped into his mind most every day now. He found himself imagining going home at the end of the day and spending the evening, not with Mum and Pa, but with Ann. Such thoughts used to scare him. Now they beckoned to him.

With Ann, it was a foregone conclusion they would get married. She was just waiting for James to catch up. She first had such thoughts back in the mumblety-peg days. Of course, she said nothing to anyone, thinking it was just a young girls crush, but each time they crossed paths in the years since, the feelings were reinforced. She had been courted by others, with her long hair, womanly figure, bright eyes, and a quick smile. Each time she would mentally compare the two men, James, and the would-be suitor. There were even two proposals for marriage in the last six months. Her response was an abrupt refusal and an end to the courtship of that suitor.

The only thing that troubled her now was her new job. With the new machines, she had gone from being one of nearly 500 workers to one of 15 workers. Since the machines were new to everyone, there was no predetermined pecking order. David had let the employees know when they started back up, he was being promoted to General Superintendent, meaning, he would move off the floor to an office and they'd be looking for one of the workers to become floor foreman or foreperson. The main goal of such a person would be to maximize efficiency and production of the floor. They would not only help run their mule but watch over the operation of the other two mules. This person would also have the authority to fire anyone they deemed lacking in their duties, and hire and train new people as needed.

The appointment of the new foreman was still a couple of months off. Ann felt like she had an excellent chance of being selected, but marriage to a good provider was paramount in her mind. James had proven he could be that provider. Besides that, there was no other man she'd rather be with. She cared for him deeply and often had thoughts of spending the rest of their lives together. Ann had been content to let James take his time aligning his desires with hers, but now she felt pressure at the mill as she waited to see who would be chosen as foreman. The question that kept swirling around in her mind, as the two of them lazily stared into the fire was; would it be weeks or months or years before James would be ready to propose?

The silent pauses between comments were long, but the quiet belied the whirlwind of thoughts racing through each of their minds. Ann's thoughts were around the balancing act of work, promotion, and marriage to James. James' thoughts were around planning for a home, providing for Ann and even occasional thoughts about the family that would follow. That led to thoughts of being a father, of not only providing for but of raising and teaching his children. His Children! The thought jolted him.

It wasn't long before he circled back and thoughts of his children were again on his mind. Like touching a hot stove, he recoiled when he reflected on "his children". But as these thoughts reoccurred, he found he liked the idea. Gradually he embraced the idea. Considering Ann as his wife held high appeal. Before they left their favorite spot that evening to return to the mundane chore of anticipating another week of work in the mine or at the mill, each resolved to step firmly towards a life together. Specifically for James, that meant a proposal. Where? When? How?

CHAPTER
34

Monday mornings were a massive let down for both. Neither of them disliked their work. They enjoyed their work and the challenge. But work ranked a distance second place to spending the day together. The time they spent together was their fairytale time. Work was back to reality, earning a living, putting food on the table and clothes on their backs.

For James, the routine of working the levers and pedals of his machine had become so engrained he would work for hours without thinking about the motions he was carrying out. As a diversion, he would sometimes concentrate on the movements of the bucket to see if he could improve the time it took between bucket dumps by a fraction of a second.

However, this Monday morning, James was distracted. It was an anxious, but pleasurable distraction. He had decided to ask Ann to marry him. The distraction was, when and how should he ask her?

James was well aware of Ann's potential of becoming the floor foreman. He also determined his income was sufficient so she wouldn't have to work at the mill. He was pleased by the fact that they had selected her to be one of the few that was kept on when they installed the new machines. Also by the possibility she would be chosen as the new floor foreman. That was no small item considering the hundreds that used to work on her floor, and now there were only a few.

"What have you got on your mind, James?" asked his mother that night after supper. It was April, still cold enough at night to have a fire going. James was making an occasional whittle stroke on a leg for a new chair. His mother was sewing up another hole that had appeared in one of Joshua's socks. "You haven't said five words all night tonight. Was there anything wrong at the mine today?" Again, no words from James. He just smiled and shook his head, no. "Are things alright with Ann?" His mother knew that question would get some reaction from him and get him talking. But she wasn't sure if it would be positive or negative.

"You always get right to the heart of the matter, Mum," James replied, beaming. "I've decided to ask Ann to marry me." He looked at his mother to gage her reaction.

His mother smiled, stopped her sewing and looked up at James, "I supposed as much. Your father and I think it's a great idea. We're impressed with Ann, and it appears she is very devoted to you." Joshua also was sitting by the fire, but had dozed off, mouth open and wasn't disturbed by the conversation.

"There is one problem I'm not sure how to deal with," James explained. "Ann has done well at the mill with the new machines and is being strongly considered for floor foreman. If I propose now, how will it affect her position at the mill? I don't want to make things complicated for her."

"My advice?" his mother said. "Ask her, get married and work out the situation at the mill together. Being married shouldn't change her standing at the mill." The way she emphasized "being married" said more to James than any further explanation could.

"Thanks, Mum. You always seem to know what to say." James replied.

The next Sunday, James was at Ann's by mid-day. "I'd like to take a walk today, and take a picnic," James announced when he arrived.

"That sounds good, but we always take a walk when the weather is good enough. You sound like this is going to be different," Ann questioned.

James chided himself for not being casual enough about it, but added, "I've got a different place in mind."

"Do I get a hint as to where we're going? Or am I to just blindly follow?" Ann teased.

"I guess you'll have to trust your guide," James answered, "It's a little further away than we're use to going, so pack some extra bread and cheese."

They started walking northeast, towards some of the hills surrounding Shaw. As they gained elevation, they could look down on the town and pick out their homes. Further away stood Oldham, looking like a porcupine with its hundreds of chimneys reaching skyward. The spring leaves and flowers were appearing, giving a pleasant fragrance that had been absent over the winter months. Along with the flowers, a sweet, smoky smell filled the air as homes were warmed with burning wood, instead of the rancid smell of coal smoke from the mills during the week.

"How much further are we going?" asked Ann after a few minutes' rest and looking over the town below.

"At least to that ridge ahead," replied James, motioning toward a ridge that was about a quarter mile away and a hundred feet higher.

"I'm guessing we're going to Rooden Lake," said Ann.

"There's a spot near that ridge where we can look down on the Lake on one side, or back at the town on the other," James acknowledged. "Are you hungry yet?"

CHAPTER

35

The hike to Rooden Lake gave them a beautiful view of the county. The view was excellent, but their primary interest was still each other and spending the day together. There was one other item to make the day notable.

They found the spot under the oak tree where James and Sarah had picnicked several years earlier. It provided good shade. The picnic items were spread out and calmly nibbled on as they exchanged recent events of work and family. Their hunger satisfied, the sun was high and warm, but it was early enough in the spring that flies, mosquitoes, and ants were not a bother. Big, billowy clouds floated by.

"You seem a little distracted today, James. Is there something troubling you?" Ann asked as they finished eating. In truth, Ann anticipated a proposal from James at some time but didn't allow herself the indulgence of expecting it on any given occasion to avoid the emotional peaks and valleys that would accompany such anticipation.

"I wouldn't say I'm distracted," started James, "but I do have something on my mind I want to talk to you about. I'm not good with elaborate dialogue or fancy explanations," he paused, reached out and took her hand and looked directly into her eyes.

"I love you, Ann. I want to spend the rest of my life with you." Another pause, and then, "Will you marry me?"

Ann paused momentarily, savoring the moment a young girl fantasizes about. The pause stretched on, and James was getting a bit worried as to what her answer might be. A grin slowly spreads across Ann's face, she threw her arms around him, and squealed, "Yes, I will, I absolutely will."

After they had crawled down a few steps from the emotional high they were on, James asked, "How is this going to affect your possible promotion at the mill."

Ann had already considered the various outcomes should James propose. "I'll just keep working until the promotion is announced. If I'm not the one promoted, I'll keep working until we feel I need to quit." She emphasized the word "we" to indicate decisions from now on would be made together. "If I am approached about the promotion, I'll ask for details, such as what will the specific duties include, will there be a pay increase and tell them I need to discuss it with you. We'll decide if I should accept it, or turn it down and just keep working or quit. With your increased pay due to being named bucket crew foreman, we could live on your income alone."

James nodded his agreement and said, "This is one of the things I love about you, Ann. You've thought it all through already. What you've said makes sense."

"How am I going to sleep tonight?" asked Ann as they floated home. "There is so much to think about now. It will be impossible to concentrate on work tomorrow."

As soon as the couple entered Ann's house, Mary was sweeping the floor and looked up and as they walked in. "I can see something's happen," Mary said as she looked at them with a puzzled look on her face.

A broad grin spread across Ann's face. "We're getting married," she beamed.

"Ann's getting married!" Mary shouted to everyone else in the house. Within seconds, the room was full of family, surrounding Ann and chattering like a flock of birds in the spring. James was a little intimidated by the uproar and backed out the door watching the celebration from the front step.

"Have you picked a day?" asked her father. The room went quiet, waiting for her answer.

Ann turned to look at James, a little surprised he was standing outside, "What day did we decide on?"

"June third, in about a month," was James' reply, containing a note of pride. "That's a Thursday, in the afternoon. We can work until the lunch break, get married, then take the rest of the week off for our honeymoon," James repeating the details he and Ann, mostly Ann, had worked out. "We may have to adjust a little after we talk to our bosses at work, but we think they'll be agreeable to the time off." The chattering resumed as details and questions flew around the room in a bundle of excitement.

After a few minutes, James could see that he had served his purpose for now and excused himself to leave for his home to tell his parents. As he walked, the details of the day replayed as if they were performing an encore performance. A feeling of accomplishment accompanied a sigh of relief for the near perfect chain of events that had played out.

James was grinning when he entered his home, walked over to his mother and threw his arms around her in a big hug. "Why, thank you, James. I like you too, but I get the feeling this is about more than just you being happy to see me?"

"I proposed, Mum," James simply said.

Miss Ann squealed and threw her arm around him. "We've been holding our breath. We figured it would happen sooner or later. We just didn't know when."

"What did we figure would happen?" asked Joshua as he came in from the other room where he was getting ready for bed.

James recounted the details of the day and plans for the wedding day as the three sat around the kitchen table chatting, reveling in the moment, celebrating the big step James was about to take.

The next morning, as James and Bob were walking to work, James told Bob of the plans to get married. Bob was happy for James and lost no time in spreading the news around the mine. By the time they were walking home after work, Bob was not shy in broadcasting his version of events with James and Ann. "Every good thing that's happened in your life since you were a young boy has been because of good ole' Bob, thank you very much."

James gave Bob a puzzled look, "What are you talking about, Bob?"

"The unending string of happy and prosperous events continues for James Fielding," Bob began his rant. James knew better than to encourage him in his diatribe, but it only took a questioning look from James for Bob to continue. "The recent announcement that James will marry the love of his life, the pretty Ann Henthorn, is one more evidence that your humble fellow, Bob, is the instigator, the catalyst, the key component, the puppeteer in the happiness and prosperity of my good man, James." Bob made his announcement to anyone walking nearby and even to a few curious farm animals as they walked.

"I know I'll be sorry for asking, but again, what are you talking about?" asked James.

"Recall if you will," Bob continued, "years ago, while Ann was a young, pliable child nine years of age, I wisely anticipated a potential need and desire and introduced young child Ann, to her now betrothed man, James, at the championship tournament of mumblety-peg near the river. To make a lasting impression on Ann, your humble fellow Bob, purposely lost the championship round to James, making an indelible impression on Ann's young mind."

James erupted, "You didn't throw the game. That was one of the easiest matches I've ever played."

"My point exactly. If I had applied myself, the outcome would have been the opposite of what it was. You would have lost the game, and Ann would have been yawningly unimpressed with James. Therefore, the recent wedding announcement would never have been made. I continue. James is not a bad looking fellow, but if he were to have any chance of winning the heart of the winsome Ann, he needed dramatic help, especially in two areas, a good job, and some muscles. Again enters your good man, Bob, who entices James to start work at the mine where Bob works. On that precise day and in the same tunnel as James was working, an unfortunate accident occurred pinning a miner beneath a full coal cart nearly severing his leg. James, being stationed nearby at the location Bob had asked him to work, saw the accident happen and moseyed over to render some assistance. A happy outcome ensued with no loss of life or limb."

James knew better than to argue with Bob and was enjoying listening to his version of events.

Bob continued, "Since James stumbled his way to the scene of the accident and lent his weight to a lever that was employed to lifted the cart off the leg of the trapped miner, he was offered the prosperous, plum job of bucket hoist operator after working at the mine one whole day! All this happened at the same mine where Ann's mum is a clerk in the office. So now James has met Ann's mum and spares no effort to impress her with his high-paying, muscle-building position at the mine. Some time later, another fortuitous accident at the mine; a cave-in where Ann's Pa, of all people, is severely injured and trapped on a ledge down a black-as-night hole, clinging to life. Again, James is summoned and saves her Pa in a dangerous rescue that could have resulted in the death of James and her Pa. However, James performs the daring rescue. Ann and her mum arrive on the scene just as Ann's Pa is carried out of the mine. Need I go on?"

James couldn't help but chuckle as he listened to Bob's slanted retelling of events. "It sounds to me like you're angling to be a witness at the wedding."

"It would be my honor," as Bob doffed his hat and executed an elaborate bow.

CHAPTER

36

News of the wedding announcement quickly spread through the mine and the mill. Before the end of the week, Ann was asked to stay after work a few minutes and meet with David, the newly promoted Superintendent.

"I hear congratulations are in order for your engagement to James Fielding," David started. "Do you have a date set?"

"The third of next month," Ann was beaming as she said it.

"I'm happy for you," David continued. "However, it may complicate what happens next. We were going to wait another week to make the announcement but thought it best to address it now. We were ready to announce that you've been selected to be the new floor foreman, but before we make that announcement, we need to know if you plan on continuing to work here after you're married."

Ann was delighted to hear she had been the one selected to be the new foreman. "Yes, I plan on continuing to work here after we're married," she replied.

David's smile turned into a serious, concerned expression. He continued, "The only way I know how to address this next question is to come straight to the point. Will a baby come soon after you're married?"

Ann was stunned. She had often thought about having a family with James. She looked forward to it. She felt James would be a great father. She was shocked to realize her life was already being affected, decisions made, and paths chosen by her desire to marry and have a family. "I'm..., ah..., I'm not pregnant now," she stuttered, embarrassed by having this conversation with a man, her boss.

"But a year from now, you could have a baby in your arms," David dropped a bombshell.

Ann had always dreamed of having a family, a large family. But it was always in the future, beyond her immediate consideration. David's last sentence propelled Ann into that future. She was unable to speak as she struggled to apply what David had said to her current life. After several seconds of no response, David softened a little with a slight smile returning to his face. "Talk it over with James and let me know tomorrow," he concluded.

Like a rabbit scurrying for the safety of its den, Ann quickly walked towards the office door, giving David a forced smile. She was nearly home before she stopped to find a place to sit down and took a deep breath. Reflecting on what David had asked her, realizing he hadn't referred to anything that they hadn't expected to happen eventually. What had jolted her was she hadn't expected to be faced with these kinds of decisions so soon. It had only been a few days since James had proposed and she was already being asked to make work and family decisions.

Ann didn't go straight home but made a detour by James' in hopes he would be there. She was lucky. James was home. Ann repeated what David had told her and what he had asked her. She felt much better just being able to share the conversation with James. "Let's look at this one piece at a time," said James. "It's good that you were selected to be floor foreman, but are we willing to put off the wedding because of that?"

They looked at each other, then said in unison, "No!"

Then James said, "Let's go to the next question. Are we willing to put off having children because of a job promotion? We haven't talked about having a family. Having to answer this question now, I can see why you were stunned. I can also understand why David feels they need to know. Why promote someone who may have a child within a year and quit work? Are you willing to put off having children for, say, five years to be promoted?"

This was the question at the heart of David's inquiry. Ann didn't answer immediately. James could see she was sorting through the issue. She loved her job. Ann was delighted she had been one of the workers picked to stay on. She also was gratified to be considered for floor foreman, but putting off having a family would mean delaying a significant goal. It may also mean a smaller family. It felt contrary. "I'll refuse the promotion," Ann began. That brought a smile to both their faces, signaling agreement. "I'll keep working as long as I'm able if they'll have me. It will be disappointing to see the promotion go to someone else, but that disappointment will be temporary and will be replaced by something better."

"Who turns down a promotion?" David asked when Ann told him of their decision. He wasn't angry but puzzled. "You've learned how to run these machines quicker that anyone I know."

"It isn't that I don't want the promotion. I am grateful for being considered," Ann explained. "What you said yesterday got me thinking. Who knows how long it will be before I'm expecting? When you said, 'A year from now, you could have a baby in your arms,' it stunned me. It shocked me into the realization this marriage will change my life. It may take a year or more for it to happen. But I'm excited for that change to happen. My life has been good. It will be even better when children come. I'll keep working until I can't work or you want me to leave."

David leaned back, scratched his head and said, "I guess I should be glad you've been so honest about this, so we won't have to reorganize again in a short while."

CHAPTER

37

Thursday, the third of June, eighteen hundred nineteen was the date chosen for the wedding. It was only three weeks between James' proposal and the wedding date. There were few arrangements to be made, such as a clean dress, scheduling the chapel, and arranging for a witness. James had already asked Bob to be a witness. The chapel provided the other witness. Most of the immediate family would be at the ceremony. This wedding would be considered a large wedding with both sets of parents and siblings of James and Ann in attendance. Friends were satisfied just to be included in a toast to the new couple at the local pub before or after the ceremony, or both.

As a wedding day approaches, most couples become anxious, nervous about the inevitable change about to occur or have second thoughts about going through with the ceremony. For James and Ann, the opposite was true. Each day closer, they became more excited.

On the day of the wedding, they worked until lunch, then met at James' house, which was closer to the church to change clothes. The goal was to be at the church by two o' clock and to take care of the preliminary paperwork, before the three o' clock ceremony.

The day's weather was a mix of wind and rain. After arriving at the church, hair had to be groomed back into place, and their clothes were damp from the occasional showers they encountered on the way.

Arriving at the church a few minutes after two o'clock, they found the office to fill out the needed paperwork. Behind the desk in the outer office, an older man, who appeared to be in his sixties, greeted them and asked their purpose in being there.

"I'm James Fielding, and this is Ann Henthorn. We're scheduled to be married at three o'clock," James addressed the man behind the desk. As he did so, James noted his name posted on his desk, Ralph Jackson.

"Yes. I've been expecting you," Ralph replied as he retrieved a thick book from the shelf behind his desk and started thumbing through to find the next blank record. He began his questions, "James, tell me your full name again and your occupation." As James was reciting his information, Ralph seemed to lose his place and train of thought several times, asking James to repeat the information. It was as if something James said sent his mind off into another territory, perhaps other memories and he had to refocus his thoughts back to the present. When he asked for Ann's information, he had no trouble remembering and writing down the information.

"The last information I need is the name of your witness. You have arranged for a witness?" Ralph asked.

"Yes, his name is Bob," James started. Ralph hesitated, pen poised over the book waiting, finally looking up at James with a questioning look. "Oh, you need a last name." He turned to Ann,

"What is Bob's last name?"

"Kershaw," Ann said to Ralph, and then to James, "You've been friends for over ten years, and you don't know his last name?"

"It never came up. I never needed to know it," James said rather sheepishly.

Ralph finished writing down the information, then looked up suddenly, "I remember now. It just came to me. You're James Fielding!"

"That's what I just said," James said slowly, wondering if Ralph had good enough mental ability to do this job.

Now Ralph's eyes sparkled, "And your Mum's name is Ann Fielding, and your Pa's name is Joshua Hardy!" Now James and Ann both looked bewildered. Ralph continued, "Nobody ever told you about when your Mum and Pa were married?" James continued to look puzzled and just shook his head. "That's quite a story. I was a witness at their wedding," Ralph said. "And YOU were a witness at their wedding." Ralph reached to the shelf behind his desk again and pulled down a different book of recorded marriages, and flipped it open to a page marked with a scrap of paper. "I even left this paper to mark the page." Ralph turned the book around, so it was right-side-up to James and Ann and pointed to an entry.

James and Ann studied the record. Sure enough, it showed Joshua Hardy, a weaver, and Ann Fielding, a spinster, were married at this same church the ninth of November 1797. The witnesses were Ralph Jackson and James Fielding. Their mouths dropped open. "Nobody has ever told me about this. How did this happen?" James asked. "I was only a baby, less than a year old."

Ralph chuckled as he began the story, "Your mum caused quite a stir that day. When they arrived, a friend, Jenny I think was her name, was carrying you in her arms. I was one witness, and your Uncle John was supposed to be the other witness. He was working on a farm at the time. We waited as long as we could, but he never came. The law requires there be two witnesses and the Priest said it had to be a man. He threatened to cancel the wedding, but your Mum wouldn't have it. 'James can be a witness. He's a man,' she said and mounted a very convincing argument. The Priest finally relented and performed the ceremony. Your Mum put the pen in your little hand and helped you to make your mark, just like it says there in the record book. We learned your Uncle John had been kicked by a horse and knocked out. That's why he hadn't come."

Just then, a commotion out in the chapel indicated some of the family were arriving for the ceremony.

"I'm sure your Mum can fill in more details. That was quite a day," Ralph chuckled as they moved to the chapel for the wedding.

The chapel was cavernous and cold. It would take a roaring fire to heat such a large space, and there was not enough money to buy wood for such a fire but that was accepted for this time of year. The wedding party, except the bride and groom, would keep their winter coats on during the ceremony. The robes of the Priest were sufficient to keep him warm.

As the sun periodically broke through the cloudy sky,

columns of multicolored light streamed into the chapel through the elegant stained glass windows. A stone carving of Christ on the cross was inlaid across the front of the chapel. As a child when his family attended church, James had spent a good portion of Mass contemplating the wounds portrayed on Christ's body and the trickle of blood dripping down his brow from the crown of thorns pressed down on his head. James couldn't decide if the expression on his face was one of pain and suffering or of humble submission or of abhorrence for the atrocity being committed.[12]

The bride and groom wore "Sunday best" which meant their best, clean work clothes with no patches or repair stitching showing. For Bob, it was the high point for the year. You couldn't stop him from grinning as he took credit for the marriage at every conversation both before and after the ceremony. If the conversation was long enough, he also took credit for James' position at the mine and James' part in the rescue of Ann's Pa, Jonny, from the cave-in.

For the ceremony, Ann wore a sash of white batiste fabric made by the workers at the mill for her wedding present. A wedding dress would take over six months to hand sew. There just wasn't time for that. She also wore a light blue ribbon in her hair. James wore a tie that was a gift from the workers at the mill. It was the only time in his life he'd worn a tie. From the mine, he received a shovel. A brand-new shovel. It was a practical gift. James often talked of the vegetables he helped raise in the garden.

The robes of the priest were far more ornate than the clothes of the wedding couple. Oldham was a working town. It was fitting for the wedding couple to dress in good work clothes, a fact that wasn't lost on Ann as she compared the simple way they were dressed, to the ornate robes of the Priest." I guess those are his work clothes as well," Ann thought as he worked his way through the routine and well-known recitation of admonitions and promises. Part of the ceremony was in Latin and Bob began to doze as the unfamiliar words droned on in a sing-song fashion, but his head jerked up when he recognized some English. He realized the vows part of the ceremony was approaching.

"James H Fielding, do you take Ann Henthorn to be …," the priest said as he looked directly at James.

Ann was also looking at James curious if there was any hesitation, reservation or equivocation in his response. The priest was waiting for an answer. James hesitated slightly, raised an eyebrow, then nodded emphatically as he said solidly, "I do."

"Ann Henthorn, do you take James H Fielding to be …," her heart was singing "Yes, yes, yes," through the rest of the vow.

At the conclusion of the ceremony, James took Ann in his arms and gave her a tender, lasting kiss that was not a display to meet the expectations of any accepted practice or obligation but was a celebration of reaching a milestone that started nearly ten years earlier with a game of mumblety-peg near Beal River.

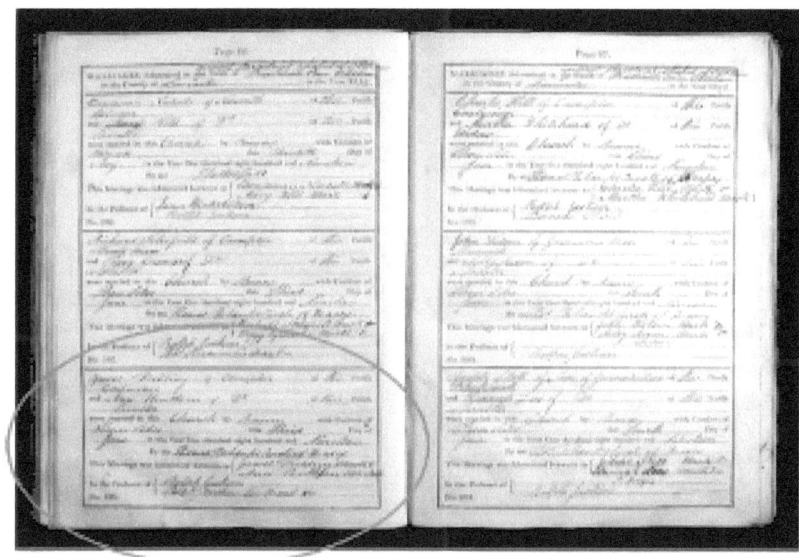

Fielding-Henthorn Marriage Record
Reproduced by kind permission of *Ancestry.com*, who own the
copyright to this image.

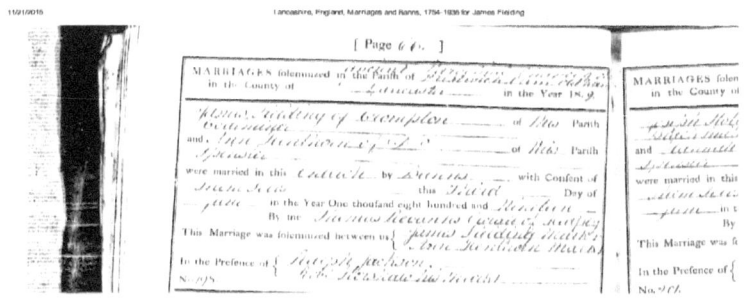

Fielding-Henthorn Marriage Record Locator
Reproduced by kind permission of *Ancestry.com*, who own the
copyright to this image.

No. 197.

James Fielding of Crompton of this Parish
Coalminer
and Ann Henthorn of Do of this Parish
Spinster
were married in this Church by Banns with Consent of
them selves this Third Day of
June in the Year One thousand eight hundred and Nineteen
By me Thomas Rebanks Curate of Deaney.
This Marriage was solemnized between us { James Fielding Mark
                                          { Ann Henthorn Mark
In the Presence of { Ralph Jackson
                   { Robt Fairhew his Mark
No. 198.

Fielding-Henthorn Marriage Record Enlarged
Reproduced by kind permission of *Ancestry.com*, who own the
copyright to this image.

CHAPTER

38

A few days after Ann had accepted James's proposal, he noticed a house he walked by every day as he went to and from work. It had been lived in for nearly 30 years by an old widower whose wife had died young. He was getting rather feeble in his old age and went to live with a daughter in Oldham. The house sat empty for several weeks. As James walked by one day on his way home from work, he noticed someone in the house.

"Hello. Is someone here?" James yelled through the open door.

"Yes, can I help you?" came the reply as a woman walked to the door from the other room.

"I'm James Fielding. I was walking by after work and noticed you here. I've seen the house has been empty for a while," James explained.

"We moved my father in with my husband and me a few weeks ago. I just came back to gather up the few remaining things," the lady said.

"Are you interested in selling it?" James asked.

Her eyes lit up, "Yes. We planned on selling it but hadn't got around to it yet, getting my father settled at our house and all. Come in and look around. It isn't much, but it might be what you're looking for. There is just under five acres of ground that goes with it."

It didn't take long for James to look at the two rooms. "Will you take a hundred pounds for it?"

The woman caught her breath and choked a little. "Yes. I mean, I think we'll accept that. I'll have to talk to my husband and father about it." Suddenly she couldn't stand still and started pacing back and forth a few steps in front of James. "Tomorrow is Saturday. I'll bring my husband back tomorrow afternoon. We can meet you here then." After a pause, the reality of the pending transaction started to sink in, "Do you have that much money?" she asked.

James just nodded, then added, "I'll be back tomorrow afternoon." A hundred pounds was about a years' wages for James, but for most in the area, it would be two or three years' wages. James had been able to save up a good sum of money, living at home with few expenses.

"Are you sure you want to move here right after getting married?" Joshua said as the little group set down a load of clothes and household items each was carrying. "There's room in our house."

"Already the walls ache because you're not there," added Miss Ann. Two chairs and a table were the only furniture James had in the house at this point.

Joshua and Miss Ann sat on the chairs while James and Ann sat on the floor.

"Why didn't you ever tell me about when you and Pa were married, about me being a witness to your wedding?" James asked.

"How did you hear about that?" Miss Ann asked with a bit of alarm.

"Ralph Jackson, at the church. He said he was also a witness at your wedding and told us the story of why I'm listed as a witness," James replied.

"I thought he looked familiar," said Miss Ann. "It was twenty years ago. I'm surprised he remembered." Now Miss Ann blushed and continued, "It was nearly a year after you were born before your Pa realized he wanted to marry me. I was embarrassed. The wedding is supposed to happen before any babies are born. That's why I never told you. Your Uncle John was expected to be a witness. But that day, just as he was hurrying to put the horses away, one spooked as John bent down to pick up something he'd dropped and the horse kicked him in the head. It knocked him out and put a big gash in his head that bled terribly. The farmer sent for the doctor to stitch him up and sent his wife to the church to tell us John was injured and too dizzy to walk. He wouldn't be at the wedding."

Miss Ann continued, "That left us short a witness for the ceremony. The priest was going to cancel the wedding, but I wouldn't have it! It had taken me nearly two years to get your Pa to the church and no telling how long it might be if he had more time to think about it. I might never have gotten him back there."

Joshua ducked his head and turned red.

"I've never argued with a priest before, but that got my blood to boiling. You are a man. If the priest insisted the witness be a man, well there you go, problem solved," Miss Ann said.

"Well, what about signing the book as a witness to the wedding? How did I do that?" James asked.

"Did Ralph show you the book where it was recorded?" Miss Ann was getting a little worked up.

"Yes, he did," James replied. "Now that I think about it, there was just a mark for you, Pa and me, and Ralph witnessed our marks.

"With a little help from your Mum, you made an excellent mark," Miss Ann answered, grinning ear to ear.

After this startling information had been absorbed by James and Ann, James asked, "Would you have backed out if you had the chance Pa?"

Joshua finally said, "I might have back then. But after thinking about it for twenty years, I can say," another pause, "definitely not. Now to change the subject, you not only own a house but are land owners. What are you going to do with all this land?"

NOTES

1 - When Ann was born in 1778, the only records kept for commoners were church records. It is conceivable that a person may have his name written down only three times in a lifetime, when born, at marriage, and at death. The spelling on the written records was at the discretion of the few who could write. This was influenced by the dialect and pronunciation of the person writing the name of the individual for the record. The dialect of the one saying the name could vary from village to village. A range of other factors were also in play, such as the amount of education of the writer, his background, were he and his parents local, and the profession of the writer's father.

Most of the records for Ann show her last name as Fielding. A few show it as Fielden. Ann's father's surname is shown as Fielden. Uncle Jim's surname is recorded as Fielden. From Ann forward, their surname is shown as Fielding.

This change in name is not isolated to the Oldham area. The same change is evident in other areas of England. However, the timeframe could be 50 to 70 years different.

2 - England would dominate the cloth making industry for years to come. The town of Oldham grew about 100,000 people and would have over 300 cotton mills.

3 - Joshua Hardy was born 1761 in Crompton, England. Another small village on the outskirts of Oldham. Ann Fielding was born

in 1778.

4 - In 1971 England converted its money to a decimal system. Before then for centuries, 1 pound = 20 shillings, 1 shilling = 12 pence or penny's.

5 - From this point on, James' monther will be called "Miss Ann". Ann Henthorn is "Ann". An Ann added later in the story will be "Annie". If this were pure fiction, no writer would impose this on his readers. The characters and names are actual. Anyone could easily be confused with all the "Ann's". It was a common name at the time and in this family. But this is also history, history tied together by fictional events.

6 - Blood transfusions had been practiced sporadically for over a hundred years. Sometimes it gave the victim new life, but often it resulted in the death of the victim. It would be discovered. The mixing of different blood types usually resulted in death, so blood transfusions were only practiced as a last resort.

7 - Rooden Lake is an actual lake located about a mile from where Joshua and Miss Ann lived. Decades later, adam would be builr on the outlet significantly increasing the size of the lake. It would eventually become the main water source for several of the small towns between the lake and Oldham.

6 - Blood transfusions had been practiced sporadically for over a hundred years. Sometimes it gave the victim new life, but often it resulted in the death of the victim. It would be discovered. The mixing of different blood types usually resulted in death, so blood transfusions were only practiced as a last resort.

7 - Rooden Lake is an actual lake located about a mile from where Joshua and Miss Ann lived. Decades later, adam would be builr on the outlet significantly increasing the size of the lake.

It would eventually become the main water source for several of the small towns between the lake and Oldham.

8 - The next few years were marked by the rapidly expanding demand for cloth, accompanied by dramatic changes in the machinery used to make the cloth. The bigger, faster, more complicated machines were driven by the steam engine, which was fueled by coal. Those who couldn't keep up with the changes in machinery lost their jobs in favor or those who had an aptitude for keeping the machines working. As many lost their jobs, there were rioters who tried to stop the changeover to machines and shut down the mills. The industrial revolution was just that; a revolution in the machinery and labor force that manufactured thread and fabric. But outside of those who lost their jobs, the benefits were incalculable. World populations welcomed the inexpensive, consistent cloth. Dressing in homespun cloth and skins was becoming the exception rather than the rule. The standard of living for many populations rose dramatically.

9 - In the early 1800s, there was no hydraulic or electric assistance for machinery such as the bucket hoist. The bucket mechanism was operated by brute force, arms working levers to raise and lower the bucket while his feet operated foot brakes on the cables.

10 - The spinning jenny was being replaced by an invention called the "mule". It had been in use in some mills for a decade. It was very controversial because of the number of people it replaced. With the spinning jenny, one person could spin eight threads at a time. With the mule, one person could spin 400 threads at a time. One person could produce the same as 50 could previously. The thread would be more consistent and worked better in the looms.

11 - While the new machines greatly increased the production of thread, it dramatically reduced the number needed to perform the work. Riots and violence ensued. Many would end up with more menial jobs, such as cooking, tending children for the wealthy, farm work or loading freight.

The improvement of looms making thread into fabric was developing into bigger, faster, more efficient machines as well. However, instead of giant, less frequent steps forward, the development of the loom was in smaller, more frequent improvements. But at the end of a decade, or several decades, the results were similar. More cloth was being produced by fewer workers. Those who were unwilling or unable to learn different skills, suffered.

12 - There had been a chapel on this site in Oldham since the 1200s when a small, simple chapel served the needs of the sparse population. The original building was torn down and replaced with a larger structure 250 years later. As the Industrial Revolution was materializing in the early 1800s and the population of Oldham was growing dramatically, the chapel was rebuilt section by section, to serve the needs of a population that had grown 12 times larger than that of the 1700s. There wasn't a time that James could remember, the building wasn't in some phase of construction, and it would continue for another ten years. The rate of construction was directly proportional to the rate of donations from the parishioners.

www.ingramcontent.com/pod-product-compliance
Lightning Source LLC
Chambersburg PA
CBHW020625110726
47899CB00002B/652